An Element of Deceit

A Sherlock Holmes Case

By

James Moffett

Paperback ISBN 978-1-78705-370-0
ePub ISBN 978-1-78705-371-7
PDF ISBN 978-1-78705-372-4

Published in the UK by MX Publishing
335 Princess Park Manor, Royal Drive,
London, N11 3GX
www.mxpublishing.co.uk

Cover design by Brian Belanger

To Amy Dawn

Contents

Chapter 1
The Failed Deduction

The wailing wind howled, fierce and unyielding. The walls creaked and groaned with force as the northern gusts billowed through London's labyrinthine streets. It was December, 1895, and the nighttime weather signaled the encroaching fingers of a most turbulent winter. Nevertheless, 221B never felt so homely and serene. At that moment, it was as if I had found myself in the safe embrace of a reassuring loved one – protecting me from the harsh realities and wickedness of the outside world.

Somewhere along the street, the gentle *clip-clop* of horse hooves passed by, as the groaning wheels of a hansom followed. It was hard to imagine anyone wandering about in that dreadful weather, let alone some poor beast urged on by its master.

In front of me, a blazing fire sputtered and cracked as a piece of coal succumbed to the roaring heat. Embers flew up in a sizzle under the mantlepiece, while the rain spattered mercilessly against the window. I was sitting comfortably on the sofa in the warm enclosure of the sitting-room, reading about the latest medical breakthroughs via a series of journals. Engrossed by the subject matter, I had failed to grasp how swiftly time had passed when the clock suddenly struck eleven.

Raising my eyes from the papers in my hand, I glanced at the window. A deep blackness lingered outside. Whether or not any lamp posts or lanterns were to be found illuminating the drenched walkways of Baker Street, the beams of light seemed to have been swallowed up by the gloom and the incessant rain. Not even the row of houses just a few yards opposite our lodgings could be discerned. At the same time, droplets stuck eagerly to the window panes, or ran winding down like an endless stream of tears – a sinister portent of the events and occurrences that were soon to unfold.

It was at that moment that I heard the distinct puffs and grunts of my companion behind me. Turning around, I noticed the bent shape of Sherlock Holmes sitting down at his desk at the other end of the room. He was leaning forward, with his head bowed down over his chest. Another exhalation was heard, followed by a white plume of smoke that rose above his imposing frame. The purple dressing gown he wore trailed behind him and splayed onto the carpet.

I had no recollection of when my friend had joined me in the sitting-room that evening, but there shortly began a series of disgruntled mutterings and concerned ramblings, whilst a clinking and scraping noise accompanied the muffled sounds of the wind and rain. It had been a series of trying weeks for my companion, accustomed to the uninterrupted flow of clients and his frequent assistance to investigations conducted by Scotland Yard. There was the disturbing incident at Kingsley Mill, the case of Lady Arabella Thomson's inquisitive butler, and the amusing exploits of Monsieur Baptiste Belmont, to name a few.

His mind, constantly engaged in thoughts and deductions, provided him with the ideal pastime and distraction for his eccentric character. All that seemed to have dissipated into a trickle of cases that had come to 221B since the previous month – a trickle which soon turned into a drought. The criminal monster seemed to falter before Sherlock Holmes's inexorable aptitude at foiling wicked deeds and handing over lawbreakers to the oft-expectant Scotland Yard inspectors. It had now taken a fearful step back into the shadows, waiting until the right time to once more haunt the streets of London.

While this situation was welcomed by all the virtuous and the genuine individuals living in this great city, it meant that I myself had to suffer the consequences; admittedly, a small price for the eradication of any unlawful transgressions but, nonetheless, an unnecessary affliction during what was supposed to be a joyous time of festivities.

Sherlock Holmes found himself in want of such diversions from the boredom of everyday life. When his mood was less tempestuous, he took to playing his violin in front of the fireplace. At other times he would curl up on the sofa in his gown and wail about the lethargy of murderers and thieves.

That evening, he seemed satisfied enough to sit down and occupy his mind with some trivial problem at hand.

Clearly, I was wrong. He kept on muttering to himself, shifting uncomfortably in the chair and voraciously taking deep draws from his pipe. I thought nothing of it and dived back into the alluring elements of medical science, by reading the introductory paragraphs to an account by Georges Gilles de la Tourette on the discovery of a neurological condition.

A few minutes into the article, Sherlock Holmes's voice broke the cozy calm within the room. An incomprehensible outburst of words rose high, almost making me drop my papers and set my heart pulsating with agitation at the sudden intrusion. Although frustrated by my companion's typical antics, I knew better than to interrupt whatever course of scientific discovery of his own he was pursuing and settled back down to my reading.

My feeble attempts to concentrate on the technical nature of the piece before me were nonetheless destined to fail miserably at the incessant interruptions by my friend. He seemed to be having an argument with himself and a most disagreeable outcome seemed imminent. He banged both hands briskly on the desk before the clinking noises and puffing sounds escalated.

Abandoning all notion of getting to the end of the article in the next half hour, I put down the papers, intent on tackling lighter reading material. Leaning forward, I picked up the first volume copy of Gissing's "Workers in the Dawn," which I had begun reading a few days prior.

The few minutes which elapsed following my settling down to continue the book proved useless. Having sifted through several pages, my friend flew into another fit of raucous exclamations, arms waving wildly about before settling back to work.

Holmes's turbulent behaviour at that moment, soon coerced me into developing a nervous disposition of my own after having had to endure such conduct for weeks on end. The incessant howls from the wind did not help in subduing my annoyance and, having lost all appetite to read, I threw the book down. An audible sigh – attempting to punctuate my current mood – escaped from my mouth before I rose from the sofa and made my way towards the bedroom.

"Not another step, Doctor," said the calm voice of Sherlock Holmes. As I paused behind him, I noticed he had kept his head bent down, but instead raised his right hand with the forefinger pointing upwards. The skin around the nail was stained with speckles of black dust.

"It would seem my presence has been acknowledged at last," I remarked, with no attempt at concealing my sarcastic tone of voice.

"Nonsense, my good Doctor," he replied. "Your presence is very much acknowledged and appreciated." He turned to face me with a distinct twinkle in his eye and a slight grin, leaving behind another mantle of smoke around the desk.

"What is it you are doing anyway?" I enquired, moving closer towards him to catch a glimpse of what lay on the desk. Besides the usual disordered state which accompanied most of my companion's sedentary analysis sessions, there lay before him a decorative tobacco pipe. From its blackened bowl a few wisps of smoke emerged, while the shank curved out rather abruptly from the chamber, before it formed into an unusually long and uneven stem. It was made of briar wood and by the worn stummel and the chewed lip where the mouth drew out the fumes of burning tobacco, it was evident that it belonged to a serious practitioner of the art.

"It's merely a distraction. Nothing more," interjected Holmes, in answer to my query. He waved his hand carelessly while rolling his half-shut eyes.

Scattered around the pipe lay cooling embers, along with a cluttered assortment of shag tobacco mixed with grey smudges of ash. A small chemical set, with test-tubes, pipettes and a magnifying lens lay within reach.

Sherlock Holmes took the tobacco-pipe in his hands.

"Yours?" I asked.

"Someone else's. But I have endeavoured to try it for myself – as an experiment of sorts." He paused and looked away, as if his thoughts had momentarily drifted off elsewhere, before returning his glance and inhaling once more from the pipe.

"Would you care to give it a go?" he asked, looking back up from behind a veil of smoke, as a slight frown clouded his face. The acrid smell invaded my nostrils. A burning sensation followed, which was accompanied by a powerful aroma common to the strongest blends of tobacco and yet altogether distinct. Exotic in its scent, it left a bitter taste on the tongue once breathed in through the nose.

Glancing at my appalled expression, Holmes placed the pipe back onto the desk before facing me once again with a smile.

"I do apologise for having distracted you from your medical journals. I was in the midst of conducting a curious little analysis of this object before my sudden frustration prevented you from indulging in some further reading of Gissing's book."

My mind briefly recalled those last few minutes on the sofa. Neither during my journal reading, nor when I had picked up the book, had Holmes turned round to take note of my actions. How he had arrived at such a precise statement of facts was beyond me, but I had little doubt that once he ended up explaining it all, it would seem most obvious when the process of reasoning was divulged.

I spoke no word, but the subtle smile which formed round my mouth was enough indication for my companion to notice and understand. I did not encourage an explanation, although I desired one. He knew that and obliged with his typical keenness to demonstrate his skill of thought.

"Any process of deduction, when applied to its full potential, makes use of every one of the senses at our disposal, assessing the relevance of each depending on the situation one is in. I could not see you with my back turned towards you. Thus, I employed the use of my hearing in order to comprehend your actions."

He shifted in his chair, relishing my intrigued expression, before he continued.

"Paper has a very unusual auditory quality to it. It is sharp, crisp and quite distinct. Medical journals, on the other hand, which in all probability only a medical man would venture to read on a night like this, require careful study and understanding. Your hesitation and difficulty in comprehending the subject was characterised by the lack of paper shuffling when turning a page. The disparity in behaviour later on, was inescapable. No sooner had you put down the journals and taken hold of the book did it emerge to my auditory faculties that this was a more uncomplicated reading exercise. Clearly, this was no medical article, but something with a rather more accessible style of writing. A book of sorts then. A book which, I admit I had seen lying close by the sofa on several occasions, and which seemed the only plausible volume you would pick up after your failed attempt at tackling the journals.

"Finally, though the natural elements outside contributed to some interference in my auditory perception, no one could have failed to perceive the frustrated sigh of a tired man in need of proving a point to his friend."

Sherlock Holmes smirked at the concluding statement. He leaned back in the chair and produced another puff from that same pipe.

"As always Holmes, your interpretation is most meticulous," I admitted.

He gave a half-hearted moan, shrugging off my compliment. He turned his head away like some injured animal whose pride seemed in tatters. I thought back to his irksome behaviour at the desk.

"Is something the matter, Holmes?" I asked.

"Nothing whatsoever."

"What was the cause of your sudden annoyance back then?" I persisted.

He sighed deeply and closed his eyes, as if recalling some painful memory, before giving in to my questioning.

"There comes a time, Watson, when the workings of the mind – so accustomed to the complexities of human behaviour and exposed for such a long period to the most abstruse problems – cease abruptly, and the tedious normality of life takes over, then the brain momentarily fails to function to the best of its abilities and overlooks the most trivial of things."

"How so?" I enquired, eager to understand how Sherlock Holmes could find himself vexed by a superficial series of deductions.

He gestured towards the sofa, inviting me to sit back down. Having done so, he began his account.

"Wading through the eternal bustle of London's interminable streets, I found the observation of patterns and rituals of this city's inhabitants to be most invigorating, alleviating some of the tediousness brought upon by a lack of cases. This morning, I walked all the way through Bloomsbury and on to Farringdon, until I reached the Smithfield market. Amid that endless array of handcarts piled with meat and poultry, the cries of costermongers, and the trade and exercise of commerce, I passed by a fascinating individual. He was standing behind his cart replete with fruit and vegetables. He raised his voice above the clamour as he attempted to sell his produce. Between each attempt, he held a curious tobacco-pipe and drew several breaths from it. As the smoke rose and wafted out into the passageway, my mind was struck by the sudden distinctness of what I experienced." Holmes paused momentarily. It was unusual for him to halt in the midst of an account, yet I could see from his clouded expression that, as the memory of that moment came back to him, he attempted once more to deduce what had vexed him so much a few minutes ago.

"You mean the pipe?" I offered, as assistance for him to proceed.

"Tobacco, Watson!" He stood up from the chair and paced briskly round the sitting-room, clearly agitated. He said nothing more – bearing only an annoyed expression as he paused in front of the window, gazing outside.

I had borne witness to that same kind of attitude during some of our cases together. When the problems presented by a client became too entangled and complex for my friend to seek an instant resolution, the great figure of Sherlock Holmes seemed to stumble before the mystery itself. Yet, no matter how precarious the situation presented, he has always successfully managed to reveal the truth in the end.

The striking figure of my friend, his hands cupped behind his back staring in silence at the bustle outside, brought to me a sudden realisation that even London's greatest consulting detective was not infallible. He was a human being, a man of flesh and blood. The powerful machine would at times succumb to the pressures imposed on it by other elements.

Holmes was no different. Yet, how tobacco could have stumped my companion's deduction skills was beyond me. The story so far made no sense whatsoever. I even wondered whether the lack of recent productiveness and the weight of boredom had somehow posed a strain on my friend's mental clarity.

The wind had now lessened in force and the wailing and howling gradually subsided, giving way to the sharp pelting of rain against the window.

"I once stated to you my ability to distinguish the brand of any cigar or tobacco ash at a glance," Holmes proclaimed on a sudden. "It is a skill that I have felt both proud of and considered to be an essential art in many a riddle I have been asked to unravel."

He kept his back towards me, glancing out of the window. The drops of rain came down thick and fast against the glass panes.

"But the blend escapes me," he said, lowering his tone as if speaking to himself. He turned round, his deep clear eyes staring at me. "I've been trying to analyse it since coming back from the market." He paused, his thoughts briefly distracted and his eyes now far away. He considered for a moment and then dashed back to the desk, picking up the worn pipe.

"Once I detected its overpowering scent amid the tumult of passersby at Smithfield, I approached the costermonger and asked him for the name of the brand he used. He simply laughed it off and would not answer me. In the end, I think he took it as a sport, and unless I had anything of monetary value to offer, he would speak no more of it save to say that his supplier had particular tastes. He then blew a few more puffs in my direction as if to taunt me. The scent was so distinct and somehow familiar. In my mind, I scoured through all the types of tobacco I could recognise but was unable to identify its qualities. The fragrance and the bitterness eluded me. I found myself overthrown by a London inhabitant who sells apples and cabbages for a living.

"'You're sure as stumped sir, and that's no mistake,' giggled the costermonger's voice beside me. I turned and stared at him, and on some sudden impulse I offered him a few shillings in return for the pipe. He looked at me rather oddly but given that my generous offer far exceeded its value, he considered it a good bargain and found it impossible to refuse."

Holmes relit the pipe and produced another puff of smoke before reaching out for his lens to examine any intricacies and subtle details he may have overlooked.

"So that is what I have been doing since then," he said, glancing at me during his investigation. "I hope to be able to collect enough data on the peculiarities of this blend by smoking out any remaining tobacco leaf in its crevices, while analysing the ash produced; all the while as I compare its consistency with other brands." He bent his head again and proceeded with his observations.

Holmes's outlandish behaviour became more bizarre with every passing day. I thought the whole affair was rather absurd and futile, but it was quite useless trying to convince him otherwise or talk him out of it. Eventually, his mind would find other more sensible mysteries with which to occupy itself.

Dejected by all this, I rose from the sofa and walked across the sitting-room.

"Aren't you staying a while longer?" enquired my friend, now back at his desk.

"I am tired Holmes, and I wish to retire to my bedroom." Making my way towards the door I could not resist one final remark. "But do let me know the results of your investigation," I added, with a hint of sarcasm.

Before I had taken another step, there came a loud banging from downstairs.

A series of sharp knocks on the front door could be clearly heard. I had been lodging at 221B for a sufficient period of time to discern that the pressure applied with each knock gave considerable validity to the idea that whoever was knocking, was in some state of agitated disposition. I turned back, to find Sherlock Holmes still enraptured by the mysteries of his pipe.

Hardly a moment later, hurried footsteps seemed to traverse the apartment beneath us. We heard the front door being unlocked and Mrs. Hudson's unmistakable shriek rose from below. At the sound, Holmes raised his head from the desk. He abandoned the chair and made his way towards the door of our lodgings.

Someone was climbing up the staircase as I joined Holmes.

As he opened the door, there came into view a woman, or so she seemed. She was drenched from head to toe. Water dripped from her dark, dank hair. Her soaking dress had left a trail upon the carpet on her way up.

Her face, hidden behind tufts of wet tresses, was pale and her eyes were half-shut, worn by fear and weariness. She stopped on the landing at the top of the stairs, uncertain. Looking at both of us in turn, she stumbled and fell to the floor in a faint.

"Watson!" cried Holmes, as we both ran to her aid.

Chapter 2
The Plea of Miss Eleonora Harper

The rain had ceased in strength, but the pattering against the window persisted. The fire was now roaring as Holmes fed it with a shovelful of coal, while I attended to the medical needs of the patient.

As soon as she succumbed to a faint, Holmes and I had carefully carried her onto the sofa, with a blanket on top to warm her. Mrs. Hudson, as much perturbed by the soaking carpet as by the woman's appearance, had prepared a concoction of water and brandy on the orders of my friend, before leaving us alone with the woman.

It took a while for her to come to her senses, and by that time, the warm air from the fire had greatly assisted her condition. She winced as she opened her eyes and saw the bright light emerging from the fireplace. Although she had no fever, her pulse was weak and her face remained pale, even after sipping some of the brandy. With my diagnosis complete, I came to the conclusion that the woman was suffering from a mild onset of that condition known as hypothermia, when the temperature of the body falls below the typical level. Given her drenched aspect and the abominable weather outside, the reason for her appearance was rather obvious. Yet, upon closer inspection, I realised the top part of her head was not as wet as the rest of her hair. Undoubtedly, she had used her hands to shield herself from the rain.

As to the reasons why she had come to us so late in the evening and without care for her wellbeing, that was a different matter altogether. She was young and must have been no more than twenty-five. The dress she wore gave no indication that she came from a poor upbringing, and her swift recovery gave ample indication that she was a healthy individual as far as could be discerned. My medical experience had provided her with the necessary assistance to restore her health. What could have driven her to undertake such a perilous journey to 221B was something I could not comprehend, which is why I looked towards my friend for assistance – the only person who could now help the woman.

Holmes had taken a seat in his armchair. He rested both elbows on his knees, while keeping the tips of his fingers touching together. His face throughout this whole ordeal had remained stern and unyielding. There was no state of concern or pity in his expression, except perhaps for a faint flicker in his eyes, but it was fleeting and passed without a trace. He now sat silent, gazing at the woman lying opposite him.

I offered her the drink and she took a few more sips before clinging to my arm to be propped up on the sofa. She clung to the blanket around her, looking bleary-eyed yet regaining strength. I left her side and sat down beside my companion, eager to learn what had brought such a young woman to our lodgings.

"Whenever you are ready madam," I said, looking at her with some trepidation, while hoping she would not succumb from too much exertion. She shifted slightly and readjusted the blanket. Wiping away some dank tresses from her face, she cleared her throat and spoke.

"Thank you gentlemen," she said. Her voice was soft and clear, bearing the slightest hint of a quiver. "I owe you much for assisting me in a night such as this. Urgent need has driven me forth from my house on Warner Street and brought me all the way here to seek your assistance." The woman paused again. She reached out for the glass of brandy on the table before her and took another sip. Looking at each of us in turn, she halted her gaze on my companion.

"I believe you are the esteemed Mr. Sherlock Holmes."

"That is correct," replied my companion, leaning back in his armchair, "and who might you be, if I may ask?"

"Harper, sir. Eleonora Harper."

"Well Miss Harper, it is good to see you recovering your strength. I would now appreciate it if you could lead myself and Doctor Watson to the matter at hand." Holmes's typical cold and precise tone of voice reached out across the room to the woman, who drank once more from the glass before putting it back down almost devoid of its contents.

"A friend of mine, Lucy Ward, has gone missing," began Miss Harper, slowly.

"Missing?" interrupted Holmes.

"Yes, sir."

My friend leaned forward once more, resting his arms on his knees; his face, the epitome of seriousness and utmost concentration. The woman shifted uneasily under his intense gaze.

"The stage is yours Miss Harper, and we are your audience," he said.

"Where do I start?" she asked, faltering in her speech.

"I have found that relating events from the beginning has always been the best course of action in such circumstances," said Sherlock Holmes.

"Very well," she began. "I am a woman of humble beginnings. Indeed, my father used to work for a coal mining company. He started out as a getter in the Yorkshire coalfields, breaking down the coal and separating it from other rocks. It was a time of hardship for him and my mother. I was too young to remember much. He desperately struggled to perform the duties of the work in order to provide his family with the necessary financial means. This kept him away from home for long periods of time. However, I faintly recall some occasions when he would come back from work, exhausted and unhealthy. Thankfully, fortune was kind to him, for a while.

"Gaining a perceptive mind in the trade, through long years of work, he soon rose through the ranks until he was able to start his own small mining business. My mother often spoke of his ambitious character and determined resolve, and his endeavour soon proved a considerable success. It grew to such an extent that it obliged him to move to London to further expand his enterprise. My mother and I followed him to this city, hoping for a better life. My father bought us the house on

Warner Street and, after a few weeks, life already seemed much more favourable. Although I missed the vast, soothing expanse of the Yorkshire countryside, I found London's bustling streets and relentless industrial progress rather fascinating. I still think I inherited some of my father's traits of character."

Miss Harper paused a moment and pulled the blanket closer round her shoulders, before continuing with her account.

"That was but five years ago and everything seemed to have turned out for the better. Little could I have perceived the dark cloud that hovered over the family shortly after our arrival here. Whether it was the strains of his past working days or the more taxing demands of managing his own company, my father succumbed to the pressures and passed away a month after my twenty-third year.

"My mother and I were heartbroken; she more so than I, it would seem. For less than a year had passed since that tragedy when she too died and left me alone to face the hardships of a life I had just begun to experience. I say hardships, but it was mostly a suffering of the heart. For my father's legacy had left me in a comfortable financial position. His coal company had been dissolved following his death, but I inherited our house and a sufficient amount of money.

"I became an orphan, Mr. Holmes. No wealth or material comfort can provide a person with the sustenance needed to live a wholesome life. I lacked love and friendship," Miss Harper's voice faltered. Her eyes dampened and she looked away from us.

"I found myself lost in this city," she continued, after a moment. "What I had once thought was beautiful and adventurous in London, soon turned hostile and suffocating. I had no relatives and had made no real acquaintances since moving here. It was a truly horrible feeling being out here alone, in a vast ocean of individuals who seemed more intent on making a living, and surviving the hardships of life, than enjoying and relishing life itself."

I looked at the woman before us and admired her fragile and remarkable understanding, but I also pitied her. I pitied the state she found herself in. She was detached from any human comfort which her heart so desperately sought.

Glancing over at Holmes, I could see his implacable, stern expression as if he attempted to read beyond Miss Harper's words. During the woman's account he had stared at her clasped hands for a while, before returning his gaze to her face. I myself tried to look in the same direction and attempt to identify what had caught my friend's attention.

Miss Harper was fiddling with her thin, delicate fingers as she spoke. Her right thumb and forefinger were nervously rubbing the last two digits on the left hand.

"Such dark days went on for months," she continued, "and I saw no hope of ever climbing out into the light. I even thought of returning back to Yorkshire, far away from this cold, unkind city. That is until one dreary morning last spring, I was walking along Sekforde Street in the Clerkenwell area. I had been running some errands, and my mind was consumed by thoughts of the countryside and my childhood memories, when I happened to stumble into the path of a woman. As we collided she cried out in pain.

"She looked young, a year or two younger than me, but uncouth and not at all pleased at having been bumped into. Her appearance was far from pleasing, but her face, although grimy and bruised, was charming. A light shone keenly in her eyes, yet at that moment her furious gaze was fixed on me. She admonished my carelessness, even though I apologised numerous times. She took it none too kindly but then abruptly turned and dashed inside one of the humble buildings along the street. The whole incident plagued me constantly and throughout the rest of the day I could not think of anything else, except my inattention which caused the woman distress. Such was the state of my conscience that I resolved on a second attempt to offer my pardon. I took a wicker basket with me, with some food and drink, as a token of reparation.

"I made my way back to Sekforde Street and found the place she had walked into the previous day, hoping to find her there. I knocked on the front door and the landlady, presumably, opened. After offering as good a description of the woman as I could, I was guided to a small apartment upstairs. Upon ascending, it came to my mind how that part of the city was not particularly an affluent area. Yet, on my way there, I noticed the presence of several distinguished gentleman walking by. Some of them even ventured inside the shabby dwelling I was in. It was a bizarre situation, one which made we wonder whether I had come across a woman of a less reputable type. The door I knocked on was soon flung open and there appeared a man, half dressed, who dashed past me downstairs. After him emerged the familiar face of the woman. Her expression was awash with surprise at seeing me there. It was then that I realised ..." Miss

Harper paused for a brief moment, "I understood what she was …"

"A 'fallen woman'," interjected Holmes. "That is, I believe, the less-apt term society ascribes nowadays to a woman pursuing such a profession."

"Yes, but she proved herself to be as respectable and courteous as any lady," Miss Harper added quickly. "She was also my friend." Our client closed her eyes and took a deep breath. Clearly, some memory or other sprang to mind. She sat silent for a few minutes before she continued.

"I offered my apologies once more, along with the wicker basket. She seemed to be in a better mood than the day before, for she accepted both and introduced herself as Lucy Ward. I soon discovered she was in a similar situation as myself, alone in a vast, suffocating city. Unlike myself, however, she had to resort to such a profession in order to make a living. It has always intrigued me how two people, with different social backgrounds and attitudes could find solace in each other. Suffice to say, a friendship slowly bloomed between the two of us, and has strengthened itself over the last few months. I no longer found myself seeking refuge in the countryside, and living in London became as bearable as ever.

During this time I never asked her about her work, even though I could see that this profession brought her some modest gain. She was independent and her own woman. She took care of her own business and was content, even though she often spoke of her aspirations to me.

"I felt liberated. I could finally speak to someone who understood me and shared the same ideas. I cared not for people's unfriendly stares as they gazed at such an unlikely friendship. It looked as if fate had finally granted me some kindness."

Miss Harper inhaled deeply and proceeded with her account.

"That is when we come to the incident of her disappearance. Not two days ago we had agreed to meet for our usual stroll along Farringdon Lane. It is a quiet area where most of our time is spent talking and dreaming of a better future for ourselves. But alas! I spent the whole morning waiting for her without any news. At first I thought she had been caught up in some other task, but even after having gone to her house in Sekforde Street, no one answered her door and the landlady had heard no news of her since the day before.

"My concern swiftly turned into terrible agitation. I did not know where to go or who to ask about my friend's whereabouts. I barely slept, and her well-being was constantly on my mind. It so happened that just a few hours ago, whilst at home pondering in anguish at this misfortune, a letter was left for me outside the front door. It was a rough scribble but addressed to me, and spoke no endearing words about my friendship with Lucy. Vain threats and old nonsense I should say."

"Would you happen to have this letter with you, now?" I asked, leaning forward.

"I am afraid I burnt it," she said timidly. I glanced at Holmes and could see him wincing at Miss Harper's statement. "Or, at least most of it," she added, as she produced a fragment of scorched paper from under the blanket. "I was so scared and confused by what had happened that I saw the letter as nothing more than a grotesque joke. As the flames began to consume it, I thought of the assistance Mr. Holmes might provide, and realised my mistake. By the time I snatched the letter out of the fireplace, this was all that remained."

I took the piece of paper in my hand and looked at it. The charred remains consisted of the lower right corner of a letter.

As Miss Harper had said, besides the dark mark of seared paper, a faint scribble was discernible. It ran thus:

... no more intrusions. The day may come when you yourself shall not wake up to a new dawn.
– A.S.

"A joke though I thought it was, it put too much a strain on my anxious thoughts."

Miss Harper paused momentarily and sighed.

"And that, is why I came to you gentlemen. No horrible weather could prevent me from seeking out what has happened to my friend. My dear, dear friend." she trailed off into a gentle sob.

Holmes remained seated and motionless. Throughout the whole account, he had not spoken nor asked any question as was his typical way of conducting an analysis. Instead, he stared hard at our client, contemplating some course of action in response to the account we had just heard.

I found the whole affair to be rather odd and sad. Here was a woman who, just as she was beginning to find a foothold in life, found that her best and only friend had suddenly disappeared. Not only that, but she was also being subjected to further unwanted distress by this prank.

"Are you sure Miss Ward has not simply left the city and gone elsewhere?" Holmes's voice finally broke in. "It does often happen that women of such profession seek alternative business opportunities in different parts of the city. As for the letter, which may have contained relevant data, you have unfortunately destroyed it," he said, snatching the burnt fragment from my hand. "Although it does not appear to bear any significance to Miss Ward's whereabouts." Holmes paused, his gaze momentarily fixed on the piece of paper.

"Though its sudden emergence has been most timely," he muttered to himself.

Miss Harper looked at my friend with a horrified expression. Clearly, the thought had not yet entered her mind, until Holmes had raised the suggestion.

"No ... no," she replied, stricken. "Absolutely not. Lucy would not do that without any word. Say what you will Mr. Holmes, but in these few months since our acquaintance, we have become firm friends and not likely to put such a relationship aside without a valid reason."

"I admire your strength and confidence," said Holmes. "In the meantime, could you enlighten us as to the initials *A.S.* in the letter?"

"No, I have no idea whatsoever, Mr. Holmes. As I said, I think the presence of the letter is nothing more than a joke."

"Most intriguing," he said, his eyes still fixed on the fragment. "Very well Miss Harper. I shall take your case," said Holmes after a while, as he rose from the armchair. "Now, do let me fetch you a cab back home. We shall pick up the trails of this case first thing tomorrow."

As my friend bid our client a good night, I escorted her downstairs and saw her safely into the cab. Although both wind and rain had subsided, it was nonetheless unwise to journey through the streets at that time of night. The cold air was bitter and so, as Miss Harper made her way back to Warner Street, I welcomed once more the warm comfort of our sitting-room. I found Holmes in deep thought, standing beside the mantlepiece. He had lit up his briar pipe and he held the fragment of letter that had been presented to us by our client.

"What do you make of this case then, Holmes?" I asked. He looked up, somewhat dazed, as if I had just broken his chain of thought.

"The writing is of a most singular aspect. The way each elongated letter slants points towards some irregularity in the writer's hand or arm," he replied. "Undoubtedly some dark resolve awaits us at the end of this case."

"How so?" I enquired.

Holmes sighed and sat back down in his armchair.

"Why burn the one letter which would have led us straight to the mystery of a potential suspect in the disappearance of Miss Lucy Ward?" he asked.

"So you don't think it was a prank, this warning she received?"

"Not at all," replied Holmes. "I think this is a most serious threat to our client, and we must work quickly to solve the riddle and expose the culprits. We shall begin our investigations early in the morning. The game is afoot."

Chapter 3
The Case Commences

The following morning I woke up to discover the outline of Sherlock Holmes standing beside the bed, looming over me. Faint light filtered through the curtained window behind him, enveloping his entire frame and casting a sinister shadow on the sheets. Even in that dimness, however, one could discern the familiar aquiline features of my friend's face as his head turned away from me.

I strove to raise myself up, wincing at the stiffness in my arms and legs. Meanwhile, the door to the room was open and a pungent smell of tobacco wafted inside.

"Have you been smoking, Holmes?" I uttered, struggling to keep my eyes open.

"Profusely," he replied, "I have been assessing."

He remained silent, staring into nothingness, as if his thoughts drifted far beyond the smoke-filled lodgings of 221B.

My mind was still in a state of disorientation and as such, I felt incapable of maintaining the conversation any further for the time being. Eventually, as my eyes adjusted to the gloom around me, I noticed Holmes already had his dark overcoat and gloves on.

"Come Watson! Miss Harper will be expecting us," he said, walking out of the room with brisk agility.

With clouded thoughts, I failed to comprehend the meaning behind my friend's summons, until the unusual events of the night before flooded back into my head. The image of our distressed client, standing soaking wet on the doorstep, brought to mind the circumstances which had driven her there in such abysmal weather.

I quickly staggered out of bed, dressed and took what little breakfast my hasty friend allowed, before stepping outside into the damp chill which overwhelmed London that day.

Both rain and wind had ceased altogether, though Baker Street lay drenched, with puddles of water and slippery cobblestones. Overhead, from lampposts and window sills, dripped the last remaining droplets from the night before, falling unceasingly onto the pavement slabs.

The bustle of the street was shrouded in a fine cloud of thin fog. Strollers wrapped their scarfs tightly round their necks, while hats were brought down low over their heads. Plumes of white vapour emerged from passersby as their breath escaped into the crisp and cold air.

As I stood on the doorstep, fastening my coat, a low murmur seemed to have settled. Cabs clattered by and numerous pedestrians walked to and fro, filling the street with much coming and going. The clamour was discernible, and yet, it all seemed muted. It was as if everything were reeling from the night's storm and everyone passed by quietly on their business without any intention of upsetting the eerie tranquillity.

"Watson!" came the voice of Holmes, breaking the hushed stillness. His head was peering from the inside of a cab which had stopped with a splash in front of 221B. On his face was a subtle smile which conveyed nothing else but the exciting prospect of a fruitful day on a new case.

I climbed in and we soon made our way to Warner Street, where Miss Eleonora Harper's apartment was to be found.

"What do you think of this case then, Holmes?" I asked, after we had rattled along the grey streets in silence for several minutes.

"Hush Watson. Now is not the time." My friend sat gracefully, leaning his head towards one of the windows. "Now is the time to observe London, its people and their movements," he continued. "Look how marvellously the world of this great city flows by. It stimulates the mind and invigorates the senses to merely inspect the daily morning routines of individuals."

He said no more at that point, and the silence returned to accompany us for the rest of the journey.

I myself looked out of the window as we wormed through the meandering streets. Much of the scenes witnessed in Baker Street that morning were also discernible on our way eastwards through the city. The fog had spread throughout the alleys and lanes, there to linger ominously around the crowds now gathered in every street. Yet, even on that grey and oppressive day, one could not help but sense the festive atmosphere which impressed itself upon the people.

Christmas was less than two weeks away, and a flurry of activities was taking place near Regent's Park and along Euston Road. As the cab turned due southeast into King's Cross Road, we saw hawkers setting up carts at every corner, selling roasted chestnuts, turkeys, brandy and other produce to eager consumers. The sight made me smile, eager with anticipation at the approach of such a special time of year. Were it not for the strange case which was brought to us the previous day, lingering at the back of my mind, our journey through those streets would have been a pleasant outing, no matter how gloomily the weather presented itself.

I glanced back at Holmes, who still had his eyes on the world outside. He too bore a smile which looked more akin to a smirk. Having said that, I can assure the reader with the utmost of certainties that, unlike mine, his joy was in the clinical observation and statistical evaluation of the city's inhabitants, which provided some obscure finding to his mechanical mind.

Within half an hour we arrived at our destination and, once again, stepped out into the bitter cold air.

Warner Street was pleasant enough, with its high-storied brick buildings, lavish facades and decorative fence railings, as if to accentuate the area's affluent disposition. We walked a few paces down the road until we reached the house at No. 14 – as indicated by the note Holmes had scribbled the previous night, following our client's instructions. Walking through the front garden and ascending a short flight of steps, we came to a broad, chestnut-brown door with a large golden brass knocker at its centre. Two firm knocks from Holmes brought out a servant, a young woman, who unlocked the door and ushered us inside to where Miss Harper was expecting us.

Having retreated from the cold into the warm hall of the house, one could not fail to notice the richly decorated Persian carpets on the floor, the fine craftsmanship of cabinets and frames affixed to the walls, and even the overall impression of a clean and well-maintained dwelling. Miss Harper had not underestimated the success of her father's coal mining business. The lavish style of the exterior of the building seemed also to have permeated inside. It was by no means an excessive display of refined splendour, but one could clearly grasp the fact that the owner of the house was someone who lived in opulence. In our brief introduction, our client had not appeared to demonstrate any such grandiose taste, which led me to assume that much of what I saw in that house, was but the remnants of her previous life when still under the protection of her parents.

Holmes walked in front of me as we passed through the main hall. He glanced from side to side, occasionally eyeing some small detail along the way, while he kept his hands behind his back and followed the servant into the parlour.

Miss Harper was sitting down beside a roaring fire. The haggard features which had overwhelmed her face the previous night had almost vanished. A slight paleness to her skin was still visible – no doubt a result of the recovery process.

She smiled as she saw us come in and invited us to sit down.

"Gentleman please," she said, in a soft soothing voice, "thank you for coming."

"How are you Miss Harper? I trust you are feeling better," I asked, as I sat down beside Holmes, who in turn had remained silent during our welcome.

"Much better Doctor Watson. I must ask your pardon for such a rash intrusion last night, and I would like to extend my gratitude for providing your medical assistance."

"Miss Harper, we have come here to see to your request," interjected Holmes. "As explained in the telegram I sent you this morning, if we are to begin this investigation into the disappearance of Miss Lucy Ward, it is imperative that we conduct such enquiries from their source. From there, we shall be able to lay our course ahead and follow the trail link by link until we arrive at the resolution of the mystery itself."

Holmes shifted slightly in his chair.

"Tell me, where did you find the note you told us about, which contained the threatening message?"

"The letter?" said Miss Harper, looking somewhat confused. "You think this is related to Lucy's disappearance?"

"Perhaps." replied Holmes. "One must never overlook details, no matter how trivial they may appear. We must exhaust every possible clue in such delicate circumstances. Therefore, the letter if you please," added Holmes with renewed persistence, "precisely where was it found?"

"Just outside the front door," replied the young woman, rising from her chair and walking out of the parlour. We followed her back along the corridor. Opening the main door, she pointed at the top step of the flight leading to the front of the house. The tiled stair was slightly cracked and weathered, but its intricate floral design was a fitting embellishment to the lavish style of the house.

Holmes followed Miss Harper's direction and fell to his knees on the drenched steps, bending over with his magnifying glass. After a few minutes of silence and intense analysis, Holmes's voice rose once again.

"Who was it that found the letter?" he said.

"I myself did. Celestine Tilcott, my house servant, was out on an errand at the time," replied Miss Harper.

"Was it placed in an envelope?"

"Yes, a small one. Light brown in colour."

"Sealed?"

"No, just folded at the top."

"And the envelope? I presume that has been sent to the fire under your mantlepiece too?"

"Yes …" Miss Harper faltered, still abashed by her misjudged actions the previous evening. "It only now seems I may have made a serious error."

"An egregious one, no doubt," reciprocated Holmes. His tone of voice and brusque questioning were far from ideal.

"I do apologise, Mr. Holmes," she said, trembling slightly. "I do hope my oversight will not cause any significant trouble to your investigations."

"Let us hope not," came the cold reply of my companion. He kept his head bent down to the step during the whole exchange, without caring to look up at our client.

"Aha!" he cried on a sudden, in triumph. Rising slightly, he held up his handkerchief in his right hand holding something between his thumb and forefinger. Whatever it was, it seemed small and stuck out at an odd angle and was twisted unevenly. I bent down and found myself looking at a long piece of dirty fingernail. Judging by its thickness and overall roundness, it seemed to have fallen off from the thumb. The yellow-hued piece of keratin was stained and grimy with a dark grey substance smudged on the inside.

"It seems we have found our first link in identifying the author of the letter," said Holmes, holding the object of discovery against the light. "The graphite on the nail is indicative enough of that," he added.

"But I fail to see the relevance of this letter to my friend's disappearance," said Miss Harper suddenly. "Do you think it is important?"

"We shall see."

Holmes rose from his kneeling position and placed his lens back in his coat pocket. He also placed his handkerchief, nail and all, in his trouser pocket.

"Excellent! I think we are off to a good start," said my companion, as he prepared to leave.

"Is that all?" responded our client with some concern.

"For now," replied Holmes, rather tersely. He gave the woman a curt nod before turning swiftly round, heading towards the street.

"This is most irregular, Holmes," I objected, trying to catch up with my companion, leaving a bewildered Miss Harper standing on the doorstep. "The woman is in distress. Surely you can spare a moment or two for reassurance," I said, having then managed to maintain a steady pace alongside my friend. I felt obliged to raise my concerns over his dubious attitude towards our client.

"A woman is missing, Watson," he said. "There is no time for pleasantries or other superfluous exchanges." He looked ahead, aiming for a stationary cab a few yards down the road.

"I fear much lies amiss before us. The sooner we uncover all details of the case, the better my mind shall rest," he added.

We hailed the cab driver and soon rattled off towards our subsequent destination.

It was past 11 o'clock when we brought the cab to a halt and proceeded to walk along a narrow lane beside St James's Church in Clerkenwell. It was Holmes's intention to approach Sekforde Street on foot and examine it with due diligence. We left the lane and turned to our left, heading in a northeasterly direction into the street itself.

My first impressions of Sekforde Street left me intrigued. In appearance, it resembled many a street in London, but the exteriors of the buildings that lined both sides of the roadway – less lavish and costly than the houses in Warner Street – felt familiar and welcoming. Even the hectic life which now waded through the smoke and rattling hansoms invading the street, felt altogether different. Shouts arose as hawkers tried their luck at selling produce and other oddities. Carts passed by carrying workers towards their daily toil, while men and women of sundry ages and social status walked to and fro. One such gentleman headed inside a small coffee house which had just opened its doors, allowing for a strong aroma to mingle with the cold air sweeping towards us.

"Come Holmes! According to Miss Harper, Lucy Ward's house should be somewhere along here." We had been walking for a few minutes on the left side of the street and had reached a series of two-story houses with a characteristic red-brick facade. The many windows which overlooked Sekforde Street were dirty, and the fence railings on either side of the main doors were beginning to succumb to the constant wet weather. The paint was peeling off and large patches of rust were clearly visible. Yet, despite their shabby and worn appearance, the houses still maintained a degree of attraction and dignity.

"I believe it was the third building from the coffee house," I added, looking up once again at the looming buildings.

"Patience, Watson," said Sherlock Holmes. His voice was calm and his fast pace had dropped down to a gentle stroll.

"But this must be where Miss Ward lodges." I pointed at a door a few yards ahead, discerning the house number which corresponded with our client's instructions.

"None of that for now," replied my friend with a smile. He turned round to face the street itself.

"Observe," he added.

We stood there without exchanging any words. The tumult of commuters and pedestrians seemed to grow suddenly. Several more minutes passed and Holmes's gaze remained fixed – his keen eyes seemed to penetrate every thought and weigh the actions of each individual they happened to rest upon.

"There is nothing like the use of one's observational faculties to accentuate the unconventional from the commonplace," he said suddenly. "That is the subtle art of deduction."

I followed my friend's gaze and looked at the unfolding activities but failed to comprehend his meaning.

"There!" said Holmes, pointing at the other side of the street.

Before I could ask what had seized his attention, he sped off as if a sudden eagerness had consumed him – wading through the traffic and just managing to avoid being knocked over by a speeding cab.

I followed, much more cautiously, before reaching Holmes on the opposite pavement.

"My good sir!" he shouted, as he approached a man of unsavoury disposition. His dishevelled appearance, along with an overgrown grey beard, and accompanied by an overpowering smell of alcohol, was sufficient enough to convince me of the man's rough life on the city's streets. His back was bent and he held a glass bottle in his left hand, all the while as he stared towards the other side of the street, grumbling to himself.

"You seem a little too flustered, my good man," added Holmes, with unusual vigour, as he placed his hand on the man's shoulder. The latter turned round to reveal a battered bowler hat drooping over a weather-beaten face. Yet, he looked up at my friend with wide clear-grey eyes, keen and piercing – if altogether confused.

"Eh?" uttered the man gruffly, "and who be you?" He gazed at each of us in turn.

"Simply concerned individuals," said Holmes, his voice accompanied by a smile. "Would you be so kind as to tell us what has been bothering you about that door over there?" He pointed back in the direction from which we had come, directly towards the door of Lucy Ward's lodgings.

"That ain't no concern of yours, bleater," said the man, pushing aside my friend's hand which was still resting on his shoulder.

He staggered back and clenched his right fist.

"Now be off before I kick your teeth out!" He charged forward, stumbling. My friend took a gentle step backwards, before fending off the drunken punch which was directed at him. He then stopped the man's attack with a firm grip on both his attacker's shoulders, leaning closer to him.

"Such a shame," he said. "I happen to have a shilling or two I need to get rid of."

Holmes released his hold on the man and lowered his hands, before reaching out for his coat pocket and extracting some coins.

The drunkard, swaying slightly to keep a firm stand, stood silent as if weighing the situation.

"Uhm, a shilling or two," he muttered slowly, repeating to himself my friend's words, taking another swig from his bottle. "And what may you be wanting to know good sirs?" he said, raising his voice and looking at us. His weak smile uncovered a few rotten and stained teeth, while his face revealed innumerable wrinkles sculpted in the rough skin.

"Your name, to start off with," said Holmes, placing a coin in the man's outstretched hand.

"Wallace, sir. Ruddy Wallace." He looked greedily at the shilling in his grimy palm, before returning his eager glance back to my friend.

"I ask you again, Mr. Wallace," continued Holmes. "You've been staring angrily at that house's door for several minutes. What is distressing you?"

Ruddy Wallace hesitated.

"Eh, distressing?" he repeated. He looked at Sherlock Holmes and then at the money still waiting in my companion's hand.

"He comes to me, this ... this worm," he grumbled. "This foreign gentleman, if gentleman he be called. Late last night he 'ad a woman with 'im and went through that same door, but not before a-making fun o'me in front of my friends. I may 'ave been a bit dazzled by a sip, and I asks the lady a favour or two. But the worm he grabs me and topples me to the ground there, shoutin' some wicked strange words. 'arsh 'is voice was, very odd indeed. Like an animal. So he leaves me there to be laughed at by the lady, ruinin' my pride. My pride!" Wallace emphasised this last statement with a firm punch on his chest.

"I 'ad to 'elp myself to another drink to recover, you see. And I vowed a-meself to get 'im, that vile. I'll show 'im who Ruddy Wallace is. And that's what I've been a-doin' since this mornin' after a needed rest. I took up my watch just after nine."

"And you haven't seen this man since then?" asked my companion.

"Fearin' for 'is life, no doubt, the coward!" He spat on the ground, before taking another gulp from the bottle while using a sleeve to wipe his mouth.

"I see," sighed Holmes, half-heartedly. "Very well, Mr. Wallace. I thank you for your time."

He handed over the rest of the coins to an eager Mr. Wallace, before crossing the street once again. I trailed behind, as he approached the door to Lucy Ward's lodgings and knocked firmly.

The landlady who greeted us at the door resisted my friend's initial questioning on one of her tenants. She regarded us with a sinister gaze, as unwanted strangers looking for trouble. She would only speak to us on the doorstep, with the door half-shut. Yet, when Sherlock Holmes explained to her how we had been engaged by Miss Eleonora Harper, the woman's expression and attitude changed swiftly.

"Oh yes! Dear Miss Harper. She is such a darling," replied the landlady. "She came seeking her friend. Such was her anguished state. My heart went out to her, poor soul."

"What of Miss Ward? Have you heard any news since then?" asked Holmes.

"I have heard and seen naught," replied the woman, with a distasteful expression on her face.

She told us how she had suspected that her lodger was involved in a dubious profession, and that gentlemen were often seen accompanying her to her lodgings, or else enquiring after her.

"Shameful, truly shameful!" protested the woman. "Were it not for these hard days, I would have seen her out in no time and found someone else to occupy the rooms."

"And you saw no need to ask about the welfare of your lodger upon the news of her disappearance?" asked my friend.

"Why should I? So long as I receive the due payment, which I did a few days prior, I see no reason to interfere in her nefarious affairs."

"When was the last time you saw Miss Ward?"

"Let me see," she said. "Some two days ago? Yes, I believe that's right. It was last Monday evening."

"Was she alone or was there someone else with her?" asked Holmes.

The landlady paused for a moment. A frown formed on her forehead as she tried to think.

"There was a man, yes," she said slowly. "Very distinguished and polite. German, I believe he was."

"That would explain the strange words heard by our friend Wallace outside," uttered Holmes, glancing towards me, before turning his gaze back to the woman.

"Might we have a look at her rooms upstairs?"

"You may try, but she has got the key, wherever she is. I do hope she hasn't bolted off or I'll have to replace lock and all."

We followed the woman's directions upstairs, leaving her mumbling as she headed back inside her own apartment.

As we ascended, abandoning the light of day behind us, we found ourselves stumbling with each step. The darkness overwhelmed us. There was a stifling smell too. The odour of damp wood and mouldy walls assaulted our senses. Eventually, we reached the first story, and a small dusty window gave us some light to guide ourselves towards the door which led to Miss Ward's rooms.

Holmes pushed and pulled at the handle without success.

"Now what?" I whispered. "Do we really have to knock the door down?"

"Watson, ever the doubtful mind," came Holmes's reply.

He knelt down on the dusty floorboard and extracted two small, thin metal rods from the inside of his coat, before inserting them inside the lock and twisting round. After a few seconds of fiddling with the contraption, he tugged once more at the handle and opened the door.

Following this skillful display from my friend, we both walked cautiously inside.

The air, which had been stuffy in the hallway, was now suffocating. A fetid smell lingered in that dim apartment, lit only by faint rays of light coming through gaps in the front door which we had closed behind us. Dust was disturbed each time we stepped on one of the creaking floorboards.

Miss Ward's lodgings consisted of no more than three rooms. Clearly, she was not in short supply of money, for each room had been well-furnished; and besides the disordered state of the sitting room, it seemed to have been a good lodging in better times.

I followed Holmes as he slowly turned his head from one side to the other, ever observant of the odd detail which could have provided a crucial clue in his investigation. He walked forward with his arms slightly raised to his sides and reached out for a candleholder which lay on the side table next to a sagging sofa.

Half of the candle had already melted away, and remnants of wax drops were splattered all over the sitting room carpet.

Eventually, we reached the entrance to the bedroom.

It was even darker in there and was clearly the place where the stifling odour emanated from. Holmes took out a match from his pockets and struck a light. The candle in his hand soon gave out a warm, soft glow which struggled to pierce through the oppressive darkness.

Shadows swayed along the walls and the ceiling.

A small bed, flanked by a small wooden cabinet came into view.

Walking further inside, we noticed the ruffled bedsheets and a crumpled blanket. On its decorative surface, a dark patch stained the fabric.

Holmes lowered the candleholder, moved closer to the bed and leaned forward.

The glimmer of light pushed back the shadows to reveal the twisted form of a woman on the bed. She stared at us, wide-eyed and open-mouthed. I took a step back, momentarily stricken at having intruded on her repose.

She continued to stare at us, unmoving. Her skin was pale, while purple-hued veins slithered round her eyes.

The dress she wore was covered in dark blood which appeared to emerge from a deep, violent gash across the width of her neck.

Then, to my horror, I realised that Lucy Ward was lying lifeless in that den of gloom.

Chapter 4
Death in Sekforde Street

A feeling of nausea rose steadily in me as soon as the initial shock had subsided, and the image of the dead face staring back at us grew clearer in my mind. Holmes had opened the curtain in the bedroom window, and lit more candles which he found lying on the small cabinet beside the bed.

The scene that revealed itself to us became even more hideous.

With the brighter light in the room, the blood which soaked the sheets appeared as fresh as if the woman had just been struck seconds before. A few cautious and swift observations of my own seemed to show the wound from which it had gushed out had been caused by a single, swift slash from a sharp object – possibly a knife of some sort.

It is here that I am compelled to pause for a moment. I do apologise to the reader, but if this account seems lacking in certain details, it is because the memory of that day still haunts me. Used as I was to the injuries and horrors sustained by my comrades in battle, the images of brutal violence and sheer savagery on Lucy Ward have left me with a scarred memory.

Somehow, having abandoned the brutalities of war behind me, it felt inconceivable that such similar acts of bloodshed could happen to an ordinary individual in the heart of one's own city. When such a dreadful thing happens, one fears for the safety of all that is good in humanity, and a dark cloud falls heavily on one's mind.

"Watson, if you please." Holmes stood beside me, as I strove to fight off the sudden stupor that had taken hold of me at this unexpected discovery. My head throbbed with sudden viciousness and my senses were numb. I found my companion looking at me. His expression was implacable, his eyes piercing. He gestured me to take a step back, allowing him to bend down beside the bed close to the body. The magnifying glass was at the ready in his firm grasp.

It occurred to me just then, that while I stood there aghast by the sight and state of the dead woman, Holmes had already plunged into a precise display of deduction. Putting aside all matters of human sensitivity, he had charged on with the case put forward by our client, and which had now taken a significant turn in its investigation. He bent even closer, unimpeded by any sense of horror which emanated from the grave face and hideous wound.

He winced as he looked through the glass – not out of some emotional uneasiness. His was a physical discomfort.

Ever since the tragic events recounted in that small volume of adventures I compiled under the name of *The Trials of Sherlock Holmes*, my friend had suffered a persistent weakness in his eyesight. This by no means affected his superb observational skills. Indeed, his had been a swift recovery from the wounds he had sustained, but some physical flaw still held sway on him as he strained to look further and closer for the minutiae of overlooked details.

My thoughts soon shifted back to that bedroom and the cold corpse of Lucy Ward.

"Poor woman, Miss Harper will be devastated," I murmured, recalling the distressed behaviour of our client. "Perhaps we should inform her," I added, struggling in my words as I made my way towards the door.

"We should," said Holmes, "but not right now." I turned round, forcing myself to look upon my companion examining every minuscule aspect of the body.

As the nausea intensified and my vision became blurred, I staggered towards the window, hoping to be able to find relief by letting some air in. As I unlocked it, the silence was broken by the murmur of activity coming from Sekforde Street. The clatter of hansoms passing by and the voices of paperboys rising above the tumult, was a peaceful reminder of the world outside which had not yet been exposed to the ghastly scene which lay in that room.

Inhaling the fresh breeze was invigorating, but I swiftly found myself loathing having to once again face the horror that lay behind me.

In the interest of the reader and, for reasons necessary to the resolution of the case, I shall divulge a brief description of the scene.

With the cold air drifting inside, and having adapted to the dreadful image, my sense of sight and smell seemed to recover once more. As the half-dressed body lay twisted among the stained tangle of sheets, Holmes remained motionless – bending over the woman's face. The room itself was bare, except for the small wooden cabinet on the left side of the bed, along with an unadorned vanity cupboard by the window. A ruffled woollen carpet lay at the foot of the bed, while no wall hangings or other furniture could be glimpsed.

Holmes now proceeded with an intense investigation of the floor, skulking around the room with his lens, before emerging into the adjoining sitting-room. In the gloom which still lingered outside the bedroom, I seemed to perceive my friend stooping and picking up something from the floor, before proceeding with his examination through the entire length of the small apartment.

I stood by the bedroom door in silence, half-guessing my friend's movements. The breeze, which had helped me to recover, had now altogether ceased to reach the other rooms of the lodgings. The air became stifling once again, and that feeling of horror lurking in the bedroom crept up on me once again.

"Well, that concludes our business here." Holmes's voice rose as he came back towards me. "An unfortunate circumstance, no doubt. But not unexpected."

His frame emerged from the murky shadows, revealing itself gradually in the dim light. He walked past me with a slight grin as he headed towards the bedroom window. Reluctantly, I followed him back inside the room.

"Not unexpected?" I repeated, stopping beside him in front of the window.

"Certainly. Miss Harper's account was delightfully furnished with interesting details. Regrettably, the circumstances of her friend's sudden disappearance were all too indicative of one possible outcome." He sighed and looked at the body.

I kept my eyes on Holmes, noticing his facial features in the light. His concerned expression, tinged with the barest hint of pity, quickly turned into one of curiosity and amusement, as he turned his head round to face me.

"And now there is this matter," he said, his mouth forming into a solid smile.

He raised his right hand in front of me. Between his thumb and forefinger, he held another piece of broken fingernail. I was reminded of that morning's discovery at the entrance of our client's house, where Sherlock Holmes had spotted a similar fragment on the steps leading to Miss Harper's front door.

"Is this ...?" I began.

"Precisely," intervened Holmes. "While we cannot positively assure ourselves that this belongs to the same person, its presence here – upon the bedroom carpet – linked so intrinsically with the place where we found the other fingernail, is too much of a coincidence. Remember Watson. Patterns! It seems our murderer has a nervous disposition of sorts."

"How so?" I asked eagerly, finding myself distracted once again by the intriguing clues of the case.

"A fingernail does not just fall off. Both this sample and the one we found this morning have clear bite marks." He took a step forward and brought the fingernail close to my face.

"See the jagged markings here," he continued. "Not to mention the angle with which the nail was pulled out from the skin, our mysterious individual is in the habit of fiddling with his fingers. See how the piece of nail ends in a spiral at an odd angle – an indication of a sudden twisting manoeuvre." Holmes imitated the gesture by turning his hands round and breaking off an invisible nail from his right forefinger.

"The hazy picture begins to clear itself!" he ended with a triumphant cheer. There was even a distinct quickening in his stride, as he paced around the bedroom.

Were it not for the grave events of that morning, I would have thought my friend's behaviour as being most trivial. In the presence of that brutal death, I found it highly disturbing.

"Ah, but I'm forgetting," said Holmes suddenly, turning round swiftly once more as he lifted his right finger to his head.

"That!" he grinned, gesturing with his raised hand towards the cabinet by the bed, all the while keeping his eyes on me.

"Watson, if you please," he added.

I followed my friend's directions and headed towards the side of the bed, avoiding any contact with the large, blood-stained bundle which lay persistently visible in the corner of my eye. Bending down to the cabinet, as my sight adjusted to small bright spots coming from the three lit candles, I could see the rest of its surface covered with several weather-worn books and littered with cigarette ends which had fallen out of a rusty receptacle caked in ash. I saw nothing out of the ordinary, except for the strong smell of burnt tobacco merging with the musty odour of mouldy paper and melting wax.

"Well?" I asked, looking round at my companion, who had come to join me.

"Take a deep sniff and divulge your thoughts," he replied.

Startled by my friend's peculiar invitation, I leaned closer – bringing my nose above the acrid smell emanating from the receptacle – and reluctantly proceeded to inhale. An explosion of scents coursed through my senses. The severity of my nausea increased drastically. As I recoiled from the dreadful sensation, wondering what had driven me to obey Sherlock Holmes's foolish request, I perceived a familiar and unexpected smell amid that olfactory convulsion.

It was a unique odour, and yet not so. Struggling to keep hold of the world around me, my mind recalled the events of the night before. I was taken back to our lodgings in 221B, where a most baffled Holmes consulted me on the mysterious identity of a particular brand of tobacco. The strong, spicy aroma I had smelled for the first time, once again presented itself in my mind amid that ashen heap on Miss Ward's cabinet.

But that sudden thought was broken, as I reeled backwards – almost falling to the ground, were it not for my friend's strong grasp that kept me steady.

"Come Watson! I see the contents of this room is weighing heavily on you. Come to the window!" he said, as he assisted me towards the light.

"That tobacco," I struggled, as I slowly regained my balance, "is it not the same as that costermonger's brand?"

"Precisely," replied Holmes, "and it would seem our German stranger may have something to say about the matter."

"How on earth will you be able to find him?" I said, inhaling the fresh air.

"As a dog would a scent," said my friend with a smile, "by following the trail presented to us here. Come!"

He left my side and headed towards the bedroom door.

Given our discovery of the murder and the clues which were possibly the key to the culprit, we were forced to call upon Inspector Lestrade from Scotland Yard to oversee the investigation officially.

It was past noon when Holmes departed for a short time as he went to the telegram office a few streets away.

Inspector Lestrade arrived over an hour later, alighting from a cab which stopped in front of the lodgings in Sekforde Street. It was there that he found us – waiting on the slippery pavement as the daily routine of London's inhabitants proceeded unhindered.

His long, dark overcoat hung stiff over his bent frame. A scarf was wrapped around his mouth and neck, and with the addition of his bowler hat, it was quite impossible to recognise him at a distance. Even his stride was odd, cautious and altogether weak.

Behind Inspector Lestrade stood two police officers. In terms of appearance and outward character, one could not have been more aptly the opposite of the other.

The taller of the two was well-built, with a threatening bristled moustache underneath a large nose that dangled from a rough, weather-beaten face. A stalwart character no doubt, and one who gave the impression of having been in this occupation for numerous years. His whole frame undulated ever so slightly as he seemed to rock back and forth in a rhythmic, almost restless manner.

All the while, he gazed at Holmes and myself with hard-set eyes.

His companion, who stood next to him, was somewhat smaller in stature, yet his posture invoked a firm stamina to his character, with his chest brought forward and hands behind his back. He displayed a calm and confident outlook. Two clear and piercing eyes could be seen under the brim of his police helmet, while his slightly crooked nose carried a small scar. He clearly was the younger of the two, barely thirty years of age, but it seemed that his duties at Scotland Yard had brought him face to face with a good share of danger.

His complexion was fair, almost pale. Whether it was the cold weather which made his skin look pallid was unclear. However, if he had been suffering from the cold air he showed no sign of such discomfort.

"Inspector, impeccable timing!" exclaimed Holmes, walking across the pavement to greet the Scotland Yard officials.

"As per your telegram, Mr. Holmes," came the muffled voice of the Inspector. He held up the note in his trembling right hand. With the other, he tightened the scarf round his neck and mouth, staring at us with two slightly reddened eyes.

"Feeling the bitterness of the cold?" asked Holmes with a hint of a smile.

"Seeps right through my bones," he said, "and this blasted sniffle is not helping." He sniffed loudly through a blocked nose as if to prove his point. As he looked up at the building behind us, his exhausted eyes seemed to grow even more weary.

"So this is the place, is it?" said the Inspector.

"Yes, and it's a rather grim affair I'm afraid. I'll show you the way," said my friend. Inspector Lestrade mumbled a few incomprehensible words from behind his scarf.

"Right then, after you Mr. Holmes," he said, before turning round to his men. "Constables Clarke, Shaw."

The two officers trailed the Inspector and Holmes back into the building and up the stairs. I hesitated for a moment and took some time before I followed them warily inside.

Somehow, with the knowledge of what lay inside, the ascent up the stairs was easier. The horror of the bedroom still lingered in my mind, and plunging once more into that stifling darkness would be most uncomfortable, but the desire to seek the truth of this brutal murder had now hardened my resolve to see the entire case through to the end.

The others had already reached the apartment, as I climbed the empty stairs in silence. Suddenly, on my way up the final few steps, a series of strong and quickened thuds came in my direction. Out emerged the imposing tall frame of Constable Clarke, breathing heavily as he came and leant against the staircase rail. Behind him trailed Constable Shaw's young and concerned look, as he attempted to keep hold of his companion by his broad shoulders. Clarke's face, which a few minutes ago had been the epitome of a seasoned Scotland Yard officer, broke into an expression of pain and revulsion, accentuated by the pale colour of his skin – more so than that of his colleague. Old dread came back to haunt me as I perceived the cause of his sudden behaviour.

"Constable Shaw, get back here!" rose the voice of Inspector Lestrade from inside the apartment.

"Watson!" followed Holmes's voice.

Having helped the shaken constable to sit down on the topmost stair, I followed Constable Shaw back into Lucy Ward's lodgings.

The scene had changed little. The air within the sitting-room was still stuffy, and in the bedroom, besides the candles, only the feeble sunlight dispersed some of the thick shadows.

Inspector Lestrade kept himself admirably in the face of the gruesome murder. He held on to his wits and, except for the occasional wince as his eyes hovered momentarily back on the body, he maintained control of himself.

"Right, Shaw. Good to see you're still with us," he said, looking at the small, erect figure of the constable.

"So, Mr. Holmes, any ideas?" growled the Inspector, in a hoarse voice. He leaned wearily beside the window. Holding the scarf round his neck, he signalled to the constable who in turn extracted a small notebook and began to write.

"The nature of the case is a delicate one," said Holmes, stalking the room in his usual, confident stride. His gaze was stern and his eyes unflinching – a typical characteristic of his as he pondered over some great matter which steadily built itself in his mind.

"Let us take the facts in order," he began. "A distraught woman comes to seek our assistance over the disappearance of her friend. The friend fails to be present on the allotted date and time, and after a day or two of absence, she is found violently murdered in her own apartment. The night before, she is seen with a stranger who accompanies her up to these lodgings and then disappears – leaving behind him only a trail of smoke and shadows."

"What stranger?" broke in Constable Shaw, a little too eagerly perhaps. He had flipped over a new page from his notebook and paused half-way through his writing to look up at my companion.

"Indeed Holmes," scowled Inspector Lestrade, stepping away from the window. "You've not mentioned him until now. Do we have a potential suspect at hand?"

"Perhaps," said my companion, "but until we can clarify this matter further, nothing more can be said. I called you,

Inspector, due to your professionalism and capabilities in handling such procedures as these circumstances require."

Holmes smiled at the Inspector who, appreciating the remark with an evident grin, straightened himself up and cleared his throat.

"Well, quite right Mr. Holmes. Constable Shaw, let us do our work."

"In the meantime," added Holmes, "I shall proceed with my own. I will be in touch once I gain more information."

We left the two men inside the apartment as we made our way to the staircase. I crouched beside Constable Clarke who was slowly recovering.

"Feeling better my good man?" I asked quietly.

"All these years and never such a sight," he replied quietly in a deep voice. His breathing was easier as he slowly regained control of himself. "Such a sight ..." he repeated.

"Constable Clarke! Get in here and give us a hand, will you?" boomed Inspector Lestrade's voice. The constable rose up slowly, bid us farewell, and hesitantly walked back inside.

"Such is the lot of unsung heroes," said Sherlock Holmes, "but now onto our own tasks." He descended the stairs and made straight for a cab, intending to go back to Baker Street and recollect his thoughts.

"So you have a plan of attack then?" I asked, as we wormed our way through London's busy streets. I was eager to understand more of what the next phase in our investigation would be and tried to unveil anything that Holmes was willing to impart.

"Our analysis of Miss Lucy Ward's lodgings yielded two primary links in our long chain that leads us from victim to culprit; one of which is a most crucial element. The snare has already been set. We must now bide our time and wait until we forge the next link."

Following these cryptic remarks, he leaned back and closed his eyes – emphasising his need of silence until we reached our destination.

Chapter 5
The Investigation Continues

"Don't you think we should let Miss Harper know now? She is our client after all," I argued, standing impatiently beside my companion's armchair.

It was early afternoon, and we were back at 221B. Holmes had taken to his usual sedentary thinking posture, without giving any hint of reaction to my pleading. He simply embraced the peace and shut out the world around him.

As for myself, I became restless. Unable to completely dismiss the events of that morning, I was incapable of sitting comfortably while some monster prowled the streets of London uninhibited and in a murderous mood.

"This idleness will be the death of me," I moaned.

"We are not idle. We are expecting," said Holmes suddenly. "Sometimes, the best course of action is to wait. Any false step could prove disastrous in such a delicate case."

I paced the room with a fervent stride, not knowing what else to do but restrain my emotions.

"But expecting what?" I asked suddenly.

"Patience, Watson," added Holmes in a calm voice.

I was about to protest once more against my friend's unbearable behaviour, when the doorbell downstairs rang.

Up came the sound of quick furtive steps and suddenly a young boy burst into the sitting-room with brisk agility. He held a piece of paper which he handed over to my companion.

After a quick glance at its contents, Holmes handed the boy a few coins and urged him back out again.

As the messenger left our lodgings, Sherlock Holmes leaned back in his armchair and closed his eyes.

"I have feared all morning it would come to this," he said resignedly, "and now that it is finally time, I am not altogether invested in the idea."

His head dropped slightly, before looking up at me as I came to his side. His eyes sparkled with intense emotion, such as I had rarely been privy to. His expression was grave as he spoke again, "I had hoped not to pursue such action, but the demands of this case now force my hand. Such a shame," he said, as the words trailed off to a murmur.

"Good heavens Holmes! What is the matter?" I enquired with much concern.

"It is this," he said, handing me the note he had just received. "The contents may be irrelevant to you, but the meaning behind it is altogether clear to me."

I opened the note and found a rough scribble. It was not a message or a name, but an address:

> OB Imports
> Shadwell Dock Stairs
> Thames

"What's the meaning of this?" I looked back at the note to reassure myself I had not overlooked some other writing.

"That is the next link in our chain," said Holmes, rising from his armchair with brisk vigour. He seemed to have dismissed the mournful thoughts he had just expressed and strode out of the sitting room with agility. He came back, carrying his overcoat, while pushing a small leather pouch into his trouser pocket.

"Meet me here at 3 o'clock," he said, pointing a finger at the note on the table. "Time presses."

Holmes swung his overcoat, slid his arms through the sleeves and pulling it over his shoulders, made for the sitting-room door.

"You are leaving then?" I asked, rising from the armchair. My friend stayed his swift movements, as his hand hovered momentarily over the door handle before his tall frame turned round to face me. His face bore a baffled expression mixed with some profound reflection. He looked at me, but at the same time his eyes seemed to drift far away into his own world of reason and logic.

"This case is a delicate one," he said quietly, "and needs to be handled with tact. I am in need of haste." He turned back and tugged at the handle.

"But alone?" I protested, taking another step forward.

My friend looked at me once again.

"Perhaps a visit to Miss Harper would be in order," said Holmes, with a distinct twinkle in his eye. "I am sure she is in earnest to know how our investigation proceeds. As a doctor of impeccable reputation, I am confident it is within your ability to convey the sad news about her friend."

His statement threw me off balance. With the discovery of the murder that same morning, I could not comprehend how I had forgotten about our client. The comforting welcome upon stepping back into our lodgings had driven that concern out of my mind.

"It was after all your suggestion, was it not?" added Holmes, seeing me at a loss for words.

"Yes, absolutely." I concurred cautiously.

Following my friend's instructions, I wrote down the address from the note on the table. Barely had I finished scribbling, that Holmes snatched up the curious note before dashing out of the room.

The world beyond the walls of 221B was as cold and busy that afternoon as it had been in the morning. By then the sun had been completely obscured by the blanket of cloud, but the air had become less bitter. Inhaling the fresh breeze was easier on the lungs, and a firm stroll through the meandering streets helped considerably in strengthening one's frozen muscles and bones.

In my quest to seek out Miss Eleonora Harper, I had decided to walk all the way to Warner Street and help shake off those shadows of horror that still lurked at the back of my mind. It gave me some time to think through and consider how best to approach our client with the dreadful news.

Efficient and remarkable as hansom cabs can be, nothing quite surpasses appreciating the beauty of London through one's own eyes, rather than staring passively from behind a stained and foggy glass window, all within the confines of a dull and stifling cabin. The crisp air, swollen with melodic carol singing and the clatter of life filling every corner and alley, accompanied my route from Baker Street. Despite my agitation at having to confront Miss Harper with the truth, it was a pleasant journey, if somewhat time-consuming; but with more than an hour still remaining before Sherlock Holmes's assigned time for our meeting, it allowed me more time to concentrate on the task ahead.

Within half an hour, I felt sweat forming underneath the scarf wrapped round my neck. My hands and feet were warm, and a flush of heat coursed through my chest.

As I finally turned the last corner and plunged into the familiar layout of Warner Street, a gust of wind blew suddenly from the southeast.

Given the narrow breadth of the road, it was a common occurrence for even the slightest breeze to be funnelled along its length as it picked up speed, rushing out and dispersing itself into less confined areas. As soon as the surge of air struck me, an uncomfortable chill seemed to rise inside me. It was more biting than the physical discomfort of cold. It weighed heavy on the mind and soul.

I trudged forward along the row of houses, fighting off the blast of wind holding me back – almost urging me away.

A sense of duty and heavy burden struggled within me.

Eventually, however, I made my way up the recognisable steps of our client's house and knocked on the front door.

The housemaid who had greeted us in the morning was there to welcome me once again. As I stepped inside, I asked for Miss Harper's presence.

"Begging your pardon, sir. The mistress is not at home," she said, followed by a gentle curtsey.

"Will she be back soon?"

"I am afraid I do not know, sir. She did tell me she was going out for a stroll some half an hour ago. She usually passes by the garden at St. James's Church. P'raps you will find her still there."

I nodded and decided to enquire further.

"How long have you been in your mistress's employ, if I may ask?"

"Not too long, sir. P'raps two years. Very kind she was in offering me such work," said Miss Tilcott.

"What can you tell me about Miss Harper's character? Is she a good host?"

"Oh! As gentle a character as can be found nowadays," replied the housemaid in earnest. "She's ever so kind and courteous to her guests and, well, even to myself, sir. I'm very fond of her, Doctor Watson, though she is rather shy and never speaks about herself much, nor her past."

"Has she ever spoken about her family or where she came from?" I asked, sensing I could glean some more information about her whereabouts.

"None sir. And I never asked, seeing how she seemed agitated whenever one of her guests pressed her about it."

"Agitated? How so?"

"More like anguish, sir. I thought her face showed a sign of some past distress, but I never knew anything more."

I had much to think about and more ground to cover, so I thanked the woman and took leave of her, intending to pass by St. James's Church on the chance of encountering Miss Harper, before heading for the meeting place Holmes had indicated earlier.

The garden wrapped itself around an exquisitely constructed church, with its ornate architectural exterior and imposing steeple overlooking Sekforde Street.

The green lawn was enclosed by a ring of trees swaying gently in the persistent breeze. It was a peaceful corner tucked away from the busy life of the city. The rustle of leaves and branches, along with the sweet smell of long grass which rustled against the stone foundations of the building, provided some comfort to my anxious mind. A single path worked its way through the garden until it arched round the other side of the church. Except for a few wanderers relishing the silence and the natural allure of the area, no one else was there besides myself. The church door was closed and there was no sign of our client.

Just to be certain, I ventured out of the garden and roamed the surrounding alleys to make sure I had not missed her route.

Being so close to Sekforde Street, it was only normal therefore, that I found myself being uneasily drawn towards it. I passed by in an attempt to find Miss Harper, perhaps expecting to find her waiting in front of her friend's lodgings, hoping for some answers to her pressing questions. I glanced at the row of houses from a distance until my eyes rested upon the front door where Holmes and I had met with the landlady. There was no one loitering outside, and besides the typical comings and goings of pedestrians and horse-drawn carriages, our client was nowhere to be seen. Even Lestrade and his constables seemed to have completed the necessary work. I also assumed that the body of Lucy Ward had been removed.

As I was about to abandon my search, I caught a glimpse of Ruddy Wallace – that curious vagabond who seemed to have found himself content living out his days prowling the same street, while watching with a keen eye all that happened to its residents and passersby. He was still there, standing on the other side of the road with his hands behind his bent back, and seemed to be arguing with another man who looked not unlike himself in appearance.

The stranger was perhaps slightly taller due to his straightened posture. He was wearing a pair of black trousers, the colour of which had faded beyond recall by innumerable mud stains and layers of dust. Similarly, his coat had all the indications of a life lived on the rough streets.

I could not make out his face as his back was turned towards me. From underneath the battered top hat fell several long strands of thick dark hair – oily and unkempt. At that moment, Wallace seemed to raise his hands in protest, while his voice rose higher than the general commotion in the street. All the while, the other figure remained quite motionless.

The presence of that man intrigued me and I would have stayed longer to learn more about him and the argument that was taking place. However, it was almost 3 o'clock and at that moment I recalled the curious behaviour of Sherlock Holmes and his ambiguous instructions.

Taking my eyes off the two men, I made my way quickly out of Sekforde Street and called a cab, hoping to get there on time.

I had to look at least three times at my handwriting. The scribbled paper in my hands contained the address I had copied from the note which Holmes had received earlier that day:

OB Imports
Shadwell Dock Stairs
Thames

Standing at the top of a long lane that led down towards the banks of the Thames, I found myself surrounded by a different kind of activity.

Lines of enormous warehouses stretched in every direction possible, while numerous dilapidated sheds sprouted at irregular intervals beside them. A tumult of work was under way, as all sorts of labourers busied themselves with the rigorous routines demanded by the trading industry. The lane I stood in was flanked on both sides by an endless series of stacked barrels, mealie bags and wooden crates. Ropes and pulleys dangled from high towers looming over the sloping warehouse roofs, creaking under the strain of some heavy cargo fitted within large boxes, as giant cranes hoisted the contents onto some ship's deck which lay berthed on the river.

Dust and smoke stalked the Shadwell Basin in this part of London. There was a constant clinking of metal and steel, occasionally accompanied by the distinct chimes of a frigate's bell passing along the surface of the water. The air was filled with the smell of burning coal, tinged with damp wood and the sweet odour of fruits, tobacco and alcohol. I was surrounded by a diverse mixture of sights and sounds, giving me the impression that those docks were an entire world, alien from the rest of the city. The atmosphere of the festive season had been left in the cold streets behind. There was no carol singing or costermonger's wail, except for the constant shouts and grunts coming from traders and labourers, tussling with the day's tasks.

Here, beside the Thames, teemed relentless traffic upon which a substantial part of the country's commercial interests depended.

I looked once more at the faint markings left upon an old signboard attached to one of the brick walls that ringed several storehouses.

This place was certainly the right one.

With no hint of Holmes, nor any exact indication where we were to meet, I took it upon myself to see whether I could discover the location of the establishment which went under the name of OB Imports.

I followed the course of that lane, approaching the river's edge. The number on the address seemed to indicate a set of stairs leading down to the water.

Dark smoke belched from blackened chimneys which sprung out of several concealed exits. A few had been placed too low towards the ground, causing many facades to be covered by an impenetrable layer of muck and dust.

Reading the large signs hanging loosely from several walls was hard work, but eventually I stumbled upon a red-brick building right beside the water's edge. It had an intricately chiselled sign upon which the words *OB Imports* were printed in white paint, now long discoloured.

The building, consisting of three floors with a series of small, brown-stained windows running along all sides, was situated apart from the other warehouses. A low, quadrangular brick wall fenced it in, broken by a half-opened gate that overlooked the lane itself. This was a decayed metal structure, more ominous for its rusty and misshapen appearance than for its imposing frame, which repelled even the most curious of intruders.

It was now well past 3 o'clock and there was still no sign of Holmes.

The yard surrounding the building in front of me was deserted. Wisps of white smoke rose from some outlet on the rooftop, while a few fleeting shadows dashed behind some of the windows. Piles of bags left heaped against each other dotted the rough path that led from the gate to the main door. This had also been left open and a sickly yellow light emerged from within, accompanied by a roar of voices drifting out into the lane outside.

I pushed the metal frame fully open and walked cautiously across the yard. The voices grew louder and several workers came out carrying heavy sacks on their backs. I was brought to a halt by an incomprehensible fear. Some instinct or other forced me to think I was unwanted there and that my intrusion would not be welcomed. Yet, a desperate need to understand how that place could be linked to the murder of Lucy Ward, compelled me to venture further.

The men spoke rowdily to each other as they came towards me and passed by without looking at me.

Behind them trailed the distinct smell of tobacco and, as I approached the entrance, that same odour increased in its intensity.

I finally crossed the threshold and peered through the door to find a large space bustling with chaotic life.

The clutter inside was overwhelming. Crates were stacked high on top of each other, forming a series of corridors that ran the length of the building. Ropes, hooks and metal tools were left scattered on every unused surface. Oil lamps were placed to fill corners or left to hang from the walls to dispel any pressing shadows.

The storehouse was not dark, but the emanating light struggled to fight off the cloud of dust lingering in the air, and which threatened to strangle the radiant glow. A few extinguished lamps had been left to rust and gather dirt. Workers strode to and fro, busy as ants, weaving among the mazes of crates and maintaining a sense of order in that confusion.

Looking on in fascination, I staggered forward into the overpowering aroma of different blends of tobacco, but before I took another step, two powerful hands grabbed me by the shoulders and I lurched backwards.

"Got you!" bellowed a gruff voice in my ear.

With difficulty, I turned my head round to find a police constable leering at me with a wrathful expression. His thick eyebrows curved downwards, almost touching each other at the centre, while his large nose throbbed with each intake of breath.

"What be you a-thinkin' of, sneakin' in 'ere eh?" he asked, thrusting his face even closer. He had oily skin and flushed cheeks, while from beneath his helmet protruded thick curls of brown hair. His eyes, however, were clear and piercing.

"Trespassin' eh?" he asked again, as he shook me violently.

I was lost for words and my legs quivered with dismay as he pulled me inside.

"Peace! Constable!" I blurted out, as I struggled to keep up with his firm grip clutching me from behind. One of his hands was tight on my right elbow while another clasped the back of my coat.

"This is a regrettable misunderstanding!"

"A musderstanding eh?" he said, faltering in his own words. "Well, we'll see about that!" he added with a sneer.

He pushed me past bewildered workers stopping dead in their tracks to witness the interruption. I struggled, not so much to escape but to be allowed the decency of walking at my own pace. It was clear, however, that my assailant's grasp was stronger than mine. His attitude and words struck me as sinister, and he appeared to be nothing like the law-serving constable he was meant to be.

Protest as I might about my innocence, I was hurried all the way to the other side of the building. In all that commotion and sense of fear and anger, I wondered where Sherlock Holmes was. Perhaps he was still waiting outside and had failed to witness my predicament.

Whatever the cause of his delay, I was now alone in that secluded, unfamiliar place — left to fend for myself as best I could.

Chapter 6
The End of the Road

At the far end of the OB Imports storehouse was a small room that had been constructed in a corner to serve as some kind of office. Two additional walls had been erected from pieces of wood jutting out of the brick walls and meeting at an angle, in order to form a confined enclosure. A rough door had been set on one side next to a poorly constructed window. A warm light glowed from behind the murky glass, making it difficult to see what lay inside.

As we approached the nook, a tall, burly man stood in our way.

He had been standing idle by the door, scrubbing his fat, coal-smeared fingernails on his filthy waistcoat. He glowered at us from underneath the edge of a singed bowler hat, the edge of which was worn and blackened.

"Oi there! No further." He raised his right hand with its greasy palm towards us.

The bulky flesh underneath his chin wobbled with excitement as he spoke. He heaved his heavy frame from the wall, leaving the wooden planks to creak and crack in relief. The man loomed over the constable and myself, glancing at each of us in turn.

"So, what's yer business 'ere?" he growled.

"I caught this little rat by the door," replied the constable. "Tryin' to do a bit of thievin' no doubt, eh?" He shook me again as if to accentuate his accusation.

"Thievin' is it?" repeated the guard, looking at me with even more contempt. "Right. We've got the proper thing for that."

His crusty lips formed into a wide grin, revealing a set of rotten teeth. He began to roll up his sleeves, taking closer steps towards me.

"Not so fast you!" interjected the constable, letting go of me and putting himself between the guard and myself. "Where's your boss eh?"

"He 'as no concern with you. Be off!"

"You're obstructin' justice. So you either let me through or me and my boys waitin' outside will see you in a nice cell tonight," replied the constable, striding forward whilst reaching out to pull me with him.

The guard seemed to give way and strode forward to bang on the door, all the while keeping his gaze fixed upon us.

A muffled answer came from within. He clutched at the handle and peered inside, speaking in hushed tones.

As the cryptic conversation came to an end, the guard stepped back and allowed us to proceed. He stared at us with a threatening glare all the way, as he loomed by the door. At that moment, as we passed him by, I glanced up and noticed a small piece of finely-cut wood attached to the door with the words 'Otto Becker' engraved on the surface.

"OB Imports. Yes of course," I muttered, recalling once again the first line of the address that had brought me there in the first place.

"Hush Watson! The ruse is almost complete."

The sharp, furtive voice pierced the throbbing air. I almost jolted at those sudden words. There was no question that my friend's distinct voice came from beside me. I looked up but only saw the stern, red-cheeked face of the constable.

I was too baffled to make any sense of it and allowed myself to be dragged inside the office not knowing what was going to happen next.

Inside the room, I realised how significantly smaller it was. Several cabinets lined-up against the corners, with the addition of a bulky desk at the centre, did not help its cramped appearance; the clutter of papers, books, writing materials and other oddities only intensified the sense of a confined space.

A large, grimy oil lamp – not dissimilar to the ones in the storehouse – burned eagerly on one side of the desk, illuminating the surface over which a man sat hunched. His head was sunk into his shoulders as he busied himself with a nimble display of writing.

His complexion was fair, while his hair had been skillfully combed over to one side. A silky beard formed round his lean jaw and chin, and a sturdy elongated nose fell over a well-trimmed moustache. In general, his features were gentle and amiable. He was neatly dressed and gave the impression of being a sophisticated gentleman who looked no more than thirty years of age.

"What can I do for you?"

He spoke in a heavy German accent as he maintained his gaze on the refined writing.

The police constable mumbled a few incoherent words, as if caught off guard by such a distinguished young man.

"Found this thief 'ere sir," he said finally. "A-trespassin' in your storehouse he was." I was pulled forward like some condemned prisoner. I found myself unable to speak out or protest my innocence.

"Caught 'im sniffing through your produce," added the constable.

At that remark, the seated man stopped writing and raised his head. From behind a pair of wire-rimmed spectacles he looked at me with clear eyes, youthful and yet experienced. He rose from the desk and placed his hands inside his trouser pockets, walking forward with an air of defiance.

"Have you now?" he asked.

"Indeed sir," intruded the constable, taking a step forward and pulling me with him. "Found this in 'is coat."

The police officer produced a small leather pouch from his uniform pocket. He released his firm grasp on me in order to open it up, extracting some of the contents and presenting them to the man.

As soon as the pouch had been unclasped, a strong whiff of spice filled the musty air. It was the unmistakable aroma of that distinct tobacco mixture Holmes had presented me with at 221B, and the same one to be found in the apartment of Lucy Ward.

"*Tragisch!*" exclaimed the man, slipping back into his native language. He stepped forward in haste, snatching the pouch from the constable to scrutinise the refined hazel-hued flakes with greedy affection. He sniffed at the tobacco to reassure himself of the correct blend.

"My precious leaf!" he sighed, taking another sniff as if to indulge in the sensation of reverie on the smell alone.

"This is a most scandalous deed," he added, turning his glaring eyes on me. He took another step forward and came close to my face with a threatening stare.

"It would be indeed. If it were true," came a voice from behind him.

The constable straightened himself up.

The helmet came off, the false eyebrows were plucked out, the large nose was pulled away, and Sherlock Holmes's own aquiline features gazed back at me with a satisfied grin. The deceit had been successful. At least, in the matter of convincing me and the German gentleman of him being a police officer.

"*Unsinn!* What is this nonsense? Who are you?" exclaimed the startled man. He took a step back, reeling from the sudden revelation. Awash with a sense of relief, I too could not help feeling somewhat bewildered by my friend's disguise, even though he seemed to have revealed himself to me a few minutes before.

"Sherlock Holmes, pleasure." My friend stepped forward and extended his hand in greeting. The other seemed taken aback by the gesture and recoiled in alarm at the proffered hand. He slid against the desk, leaning backwards.

"Who are you? What is your business here?" he repeated in a more distressing tone. His benign features transformed into a spasm of fear, as terror filled his eyes. "Dirch! Get in here now!" he shouted, glancing at the window outside.

Above the tumult of chaos in the storehouse, it was difficult for anyone to hear his squealing voice.

Seconds passed and nobody walked into the office.

It was an extraordinary thing to witness someone who could appear so calm and in control of a situation to suddenly collapse into such a helpless state.

"Come now Mr. Becker," said Holmes. "We are only here to ask you a few questions, nothing more." He came forward once again, his hand still being offered.

"Questions? About what? I don't even know who you are." replied our host.

"Well, I think you'll find it easier to converse with us than with any inspector from Scotland Yard. Trust me, sir. They will not be as lenient as I am when I tell them to come here themselves to question you."

Otto Becker stared at both of us with suspicion, but then his tense body relaxed slightly. He raised himself up and straightened his waistcoat. He looked down at the ground and cleared his throat, before cautiously accepting my friend's firm handshake.

"Excellent!" exclaimed Sherlock Holmes. "Now, before we can continue, I must impress upon you Mr. Becker, that the conduct of Doctor Watson, here, is impeccable." He came towards me and clapped his hand on my shoulder. "Nothing of which I accused him just now is the truth, and please do forgive me Watson for my rather aggressive handling."

The merchant, still disturbed by the confrontation, waved his hand aimlessly and nodded, before plodding back to the refuge of his chair behind the desk. Holmes left my side and strode forward, putting his hands behind his back. His disguise was now completely exposed, except for the uniform which he still wore.

"Mr. Becker, what can you tell me about your rapport with Miss Lucy Ward?"

If Otto Becker had been perturbed by my friend's deception, he went into deeper befuddlement at the mention of the woman's name. His already pale skin turned white, and a nervous disposition took hold of him. He began fiddling with his papers, turning them round, shuffling them without purpose, or placing the same book from one stack to the other.

"Mr. Becker," added Holmes, after a few moments of silence, "I have it on good account that you were seen with Miss Ward yesterday evening at her apartment. Your full disclosure of the truth will aid us in the investigation of her murder."

"*Oh mein Gott!* Her murder? Who? How?" wailed Becker. He staggered up, steadying himself with one hand on the desk.

"Good. Now that we have established your acquaintance with Miss Ward, what can you tell us about last night?"

Becker unbuttoned the top of his waistcoat. Sweat formed on his forehead. His body seemed to go limp. He stepped backwards and leaned against one of the cabinets, fighting off the horror of the sudden revelation.

"*Tragisch!* Poor Lucy. Such a sweet girl," he moaned. He trudged forward and fell down in his chair with resignation.

The probability that he was the last man to see Miss Ward alive was ever-present in my mind. Yet, I must confess that in that moment I pitied him. His behaviour at the news appeared genuine enough; but then again, most clever murderers had the capacity of showing different facets, according to the situation.

Becker struggled to speak, but amid his pained breathing and constant clearing of his throat, his voice was grave and in a state of utter misery.

"I met Lucy a few weeks back. We happened to cross paths and struck up a mutual agreement between the two. A business transaction of sorts."

Becker shifted uncomfortably in his chair. He glanced furtively at Holmes and then back at the desk.

"Yesterday was one such evening. She took me to her lodgings in Sekforde Street, as usual. I left after an hour or thereabouts."

"That would explain the presence of this tobacco in her bedroom," said Holmes, raising the leather pouch.

Otto Becker nodded shyly.

"If I may say so, although we had no emotional affinity for each other – our relationship being entirely of a physical nature – the news of her death has shattered me. And yet, in a sense, it does not come as a complete surprise. She confessed to me once that some of her other clients tended to be aggressive towards her. She even believed someone had been stalking her of late."

"Did she mention anyone?" I asked dubiously.

"Only one, and by his first name. I believe it was Phineas."

"Can you shed no more light on the circumstances of her death?" asked Sherlock Holmes.

"None whatsoever. I may have trodden some dubious paths Mr. Holmes, but I only showed respect and kindness to Lucy. Her death now ..." He faltered and began to weep, before wiping away his tears with his sleeves.

He looked up at us.

"I have no more to say."

"Very well, thank you for your time," replied Holmes. He raised his hand to usher me to the door.

Confused, I stood resolute. The explanation provided by Becker was far from convincing.

Holmes caught the look on my face.

"He's telling the truth," he said.

I looked at my companion in disbelief. Hardly had Mr. Becker put forward his defence than the ever-questioning Sherlock Holmes agreed with his statement.

"Is that it?" I protested. "When have you ever relied on the word of a man you've never seen before? Where's the observation, the analysis, the doubt you place on all that is said and done before confirming whether something is true or false?"

At that moment, I felt foolish asking those questions in the presence of the two men. Indeed, I felt as if I were the stranger there and that Holmes had somehow allied himself with a murder suspect just by accepting a statement as fact.

"As I have often remarked," said Holmes, placing his hands behind his back, "a person's appearance can illuminate so much more than his words." He smiled – relishing the opportunity to restate one of his old axioms – as he made his way towards the door. "Come Watson, we have other lines of enquiry to pursue."

Still in disbelief, I felt some hesitation at leaving that room and abandoning our investigation into the man so abruptly. As much as I failed to understand the motive behind it, Sherlock Holmes's calm demeanour and keen glance were enough to convince me that any protest I raised would be futile.

With much resentment, I left the presence of that foreign merchant and followed my friend.

"In the meantime, Mr. Becker," added Holmes, pausing momentarily beside the door, "I would appreciate it if you remained in the city for the time being. I have a favour to ask of you."

He walked out, leaving the miserable man looking concerned by this remark.

We made our way back through the strong-scented warehouse, and out into the cold and clear air of the street overlooking the river. As soon as we stepped outside, Holmes pressed on with a steady pace up the lane before stopping by an elderly fisherman unloading produce onto his wooden cart. He spoke furtively with the man who, upon receiving a few coins, produced my friend's familiar coat.

Holmes removed his helmet and put the coat on over his uniform.

He had assumed the usual posture that was synonymous with his prowling of the city streets. As we walked along, he fumbled in his coat pockets and extracted his pipe.

"Now, Watson. Questions?" he asked, as we found ourselves at the intersection leading into Redcastle Close.

"Many, as a matter of fact," I uttered breathlessly, as I strode forward to keep up with my friend's hurried steps.

"But first, why let Becker go? He seems to know more than he divulged. Surely there's something else he hasn't told us. How could you be so sure he is not who we are looking for?"

"An interesting character," said Holmes, inhaling deeply on his pipe. "One who certainly hides many secrets, no doubt. Do forgive me Watson. I believe I may have caused you some unnecessary agitation earlier. I fear I have had to resort to certain unwanted decisions. Indeed, I was compelled to engage the services of the Baker Street Irregulars to follow that costermonger's footsteps in order to discover the source from which he acquired such distinct smelling tobacco. That search led to this address. A devious tactic, but a necessary one."

He paused and spoke no more, as we came to the main street and signalled to a nearby cab driver.

"Well?" I asked, as we made our way towards the hansom.

Holmes seemed to come out of some deep thought. He shook his head and removed the pipe from his mouth.

"His hands Watson," he said. "Delicate, untainted, and such well-kept fingernails."

I was struck by my friend's statement, having completely ignored this critical point. Consumed by the agitation of finding myself in an unfamiliar place, all the while in the presence of Otto Becker's discreetly mysterious attitude, I failed to look for the most obvious of facts. As ever, Holmes had picked up on the minutest of details, without being distracted by the larger matters.

The entire quest, however, had been almost a complete failure. Holmes's decision not to pursue Otto Becker's possible involvement any further had meant that a new thread in the investigation into the murder had to be picked up. The name of Phineas did not mean anything, and we had no clues as to where to begin our new line of enquiry.

"A slight impediment, nothing more," Holmes had said during our journey back.

He spoke confidently, as the cab rattled through the streets, but I could not fail to notice the barest hint of disappointment and vexation in his eyes at the turn of events.

"I spoke to Miss Harper's housemaid," my voice echoing in the hollow cab. Holmes raised his eyes from some deep thought.

"Did you now? Anything illuminating?" he asked.

"Nothing of interest to this case, though it would seem our client may have experienced some affliction sometime in her past."

Holmes inclined his head slightly and bent forward with interest.

"It's something Miss Tilcott said, about her mistress and the occasional agitation she bore," I continued.

My companion stared silently at the window, before leaning back in his seat.

"Most intriguing," he murmured, keeping his eyes fixed on the fleeting world outside. I myself tried to piece together the events of that morning, to make some sense of the case and where my friend and I might be headed.

These thoughts played in my mind as we made our way back to Baker Street.

We arrived at 221B and relished the warm air trapped inside. Mrs. Hudson was nowhere to be seen, but a clattering noise rose from a back room.

"We must rethink our strategy," said Holmes, as we ascended the stairs. I was about to enquire what he meant by this statement, but my words were cut off by the discovery of a bewildered Inspector Lestrade and the two constables, waiting for us in the sitting-room.

"Inspector! What brings you here?" said my friend with some surprise.

"Mr. Holmes," began Lestrade with some hesitation. He removed his hat and shuffled his feet, staring at both of us.

"It is Miss Eleonora Harper. She has gone missing."

Chapter 7
A Trail in the Mud

"Such is the unpredictable nature of a criminal at the height of his game," said Sherlock Holmes, walking back into the sitting-room after having pulled on his customary clothing. "It is tedious enough to follow the repetitive cycles of a perpetrator. But such a disappearance is completely unexpected."

"This is most irregular Holmes," protested Inspector Lestrade, with the air of an injured animal.

"Carefully planned no doubt, but not irregular."

"Not the case! That!" The Inspector pointed at the folded uniform and helmet in Holmes's hands as he stretched out his arms towards a flustered Constable Clarke. Lestrade glared at the police officer who timidly took the contents and stepped back beside the small yet steadfast frame of Shaw who was standing with his hands behind his back.

"You are playing too nimbly with the law, Holmes."

"Tut, tut Inspector!" said my companion, waving his hand dismissively, "if we had to waste our time wading through the petty, labyrinthine procedures of the law, we would never produce any results."

"I must protest!" cried the Inspector in a hoarse voice while stamping his feet.

"Mercy Lestrade! There are more pressing matters at hand than this trivial concern," said Holmes, snatching the clay pipe from the dusty mantlepiece and lighting its contents, "and please do not feel the need to vent your wrath upon Constable Clarke," he added. He turned round to stare at the flickering flames in the grate, then leant against the mantelpiece in silent thought. A frown was discernible upon his stern face.

I stood by the window looking at my companion, wondering what his next step would be.

The fate of Miss Eleonora Harper concerned me deeply. Her disappearance during a murder investigation forced my mind to conjure up all kinds of horrible thoughts.

Meanwhile, the Inspector, flanked by his two constables, looked impatiently at my friend.

"The game widens itself and we must lay our trap."

Holmes's quiet voice broke the tense stillness in the room, as he turned round to face the Inspector.

"What are the facts so far?" he inquired, walking over to his armchair and sitting down in his usual posture. His eyes were closed while his hands met under his square chin, each set of fingertips touching the other.

"Scarce, I'm afraid," sighed the Scotland Yard official. His impatience wore off and his face became clouded with doubt. He consulted a small, leather-bound notebook he had reached for from inside his overcoat.

"Miss Celestine Tilcott, the housemaid, told us her mistress never came back from her customary afternoon walk."

"I spoke to Miss Tilcott myself not two hours ago," I said, stepping away from the window and back towards the Inspector. "Miss Harper had just gone out. Is there reason why there should be concern at her not showing up until now?" I was hoping that this disappearance was nothing more than a misunderstanding."

The Inspector sniffed and shuffled through his notes.

"Well, it seems she found her mistress's bonnet a few streets away from the house, near Farringdon Lane. It had been trampled upon and left by the side of the road. That's what raised the alarm."

"Plenty of women in London wear a bonnet," I argued, feeling a tight sensation coiling round my throat. "What led you to believe it to be hers?"

"A small scarlet bow was found tied to the left side of the hat." The Inspector turned another page of his notebook before continuing

"Miss Tilcott revealed how her mistress wore that same bow before she left."

"Anything else?" asked Holmes, opening his eyes to stare intensely at Lestrade.

The Inspector fumbled through some empty pages.

"None so far. We shall begin an intense investigation of the area around Warner Street and Farringdon Lane. I will bring a few more officers to help with the search."

Inspector Lestrade tucked the notebook back into his overcoat pocket, before sharply reaching out for a handkerchief to block off the loud sneeze that escaped through his congested nose and mouth. Amid his sniffles, he turned round to the two constables, still squeezing the piece of cloth round his nostrils.

"Now, Shaw, you stay with me. No more loitering during work, and that's a warning." The constable, straightened himself and nodded at the pointed finger of the Inspector.

"As for you, Constable Clarke," he said, lowering his voice and taking a step closer to the pale-faced officer, who in turn timidly brushed against the side of the sofa, "no more sneaking behind my back, understood?" The Inspector's voice had risen hoarsely as he strained his neck towards Constable Clarke's tall frame. The latter shook his head and hastily hid the folded uniform and hat behind his back.

"Holmes!" added Inspector Lestrade, turning sharply. "I need your full cooperation on this. No more disguises and fiddling with the law."

"Absolutely Inspector! I shall keep you informed of any development on my part." Holmes smiled like a mischievous child. He rose rapidly from the armchair and heading for the sitting-room door, opened it. The Inspector followed him and left the room with the two constables trailing behind.

"What now Holmes? What about Miss Harper?" I asked, unable to hide the anxious tone of my voice. My friend closed the door and walked slowly back inside. His eyes were fixed upon the carpet as he approached the mantlepiece. He produced two deep puffs from his pipe and remained silent for a while.

"I have remarked that this is a delicate case," he said after some time. "Indeed, our evidence is fragmentary. All we have at our disposal are the broken fingernails found at Miss Harper's house and at the lodgings of our murdered victim, a stalker by the name of Phineas, and the presumably burnt letter bearing the initials 'A. S.' threatening our client.

"Why presumably?"

"Well, we have not seen the note with our own eyes, Watson. Where is the proof? Why burn it before coming to seek our assistance?" he sighed.

"Are you doubting the truth behind Miss Harper's statement?"

Holmes paused, checking himself before he answered.

"No, no, of course not," he said, waving away the clouds of smoke from in front of his face, "but the presence of the letter feels too contrived, too convenient ..."

He puffed furiously at the pipe, walking aimlessly around the room.

For the first time, I saw Holmes visibly flustered by the inconsistencies that were being presented to him by this mystery. He sat back down in the armchair, with his pipe still clenched between his teeth. He wiped his forehead with the palm of his hand and removed his pipe to speak.

"Perhaps I should have known what that meant? Perhaps I should have warned Miss Harper about the looming danger."

"Come Holmes! Her disappearance must not weigh on your conscience," I said, sitting down opposite him. "Surely you had no means of knowing what would befall her," I added, trying to reassure my companion.

"Perhaps not," he said resignedly, leaning back in the chair. "Then again, we must categorically substantiate the claim of Miss Harper's disappearance, or verify it as some misunderstanding.

Sherlock Holmes paused once again. He took a few further deep draws from his pipe.

"I confess Watson, the trail is weak. We must find another crucial link that will help us to solve this riddle."

"And what do you propose?"

"The murder weapon!" With a sudden turn in behaviour, as was typical of Sherlock Holmes's volatile personality, he stood back up with brisk agility. Vigour flowed through those strong limbs, while he paced wildly round the room, inhaling and puffing clouds of smoke that followed in his wake.

"It is the pivot upon which this whole case rests." He paused by the window, looking up at the grey sky which still threatened further rain.

"Given the severity of the wound inflicted upon Miss Ward, and the clean cut produced, we are looking at the possibility of a sharp weapon — something akin to a butcher's knife," he said.

"But surely the culprit will have got rid of it by now. It could be anywhere in London. The search would be fruitless." I stood up, following Holmes's rigorous strides round the armchairs and side table.

"Nonetheless, try we shall," he proclaimed, abandoning the pipe on the mantlepiece and snatching up his coat on the way towards the door. "Come Watson! Time is imperative. If we are to find Miss Harper, we must reveal the culprit's identity."

As our cab wound its way through the streets it soon became apparent that Holmes's intention was to continue his investigation from Warner Street, near Miss Eleonora Harper's house.

The wind had dropped by then, but it felt colder.

It was close to 7 o'clock and the light had by then failed. A few solitary gas street lamps glowed brightly in the darkness.

The street itself remained deserted, except for some lonely passerby seeking shelter from the bitter cold which held London in its persistent wintry grasp.

I followed Holmes as he alighted from the cab and strode along the narrow pavement towards our client's house. A warm gleam emerged from one of the windows beside the front door.

Upon the main steps we had trod that morning, partly concealed by the oncoming gloom, two police constables stood talking, their voices quivering in the cold. They glanced momentarily at my friend and nodded, before proceeding with their whispered conversation.

Sherlock Holmes paused on the bottom step and extracted his magnifying glass. His back was bent, as he crouched on the slippery ground caked with fallen leaves and mud.

Whatever he was looking for failed to show itself under his straining gaze. He puffed and sighed as he moved away a few feet from the house, all the while maintaining that same bowed posture.

I followed silently, raising the collar of my coat against the creeping cold.

Enraptured by his examination, Holmes began to remove the scarf around his neck. A few grunts escaped from his mouth as he fought to break free from the piece of fabric, before proceeding with a closer inspection of a low wall covered in moss that flanked the pavement a few paces away from the front steps of the house. "This gloom is a menace," he groaned, looking up at the street lamp looming over him as its defiant flame fought to cast off the hindering darkness.

"Anything enlightening?" I stepped beside him as he placed his lens back and wrapped the scarf once more round his neck. The analysis had been concluded.

"Hardly." His tone of voice wavered between conviction and doubt. "A mere affirmation that Miss Harper did leave her house a short while ago, and without mishap."

The statement was odd and left me lost for words.

Obvious as it may have been to everyone else, given the statement of our client's housemaid, I was unable to comprehend how my friend could determine such a fact by the simple analysis of a mud-smeared pavement.

"See Watson," said Holmes, sensing my apprehension. He pointed at two shallow impressions left in the brown sludge beside the steps. One was large, shaped almost like a ship's bow seen from above, while the other, in the likeness of a rounded square, was significantly smaller. The latter drove deeper into the mud than the one beside it.

"This is the signature of a woman's boot," he added, bending down to illustrate the details of his inspection. "Observe the distinct patterns of the sole and the heel of the shoe, with the small patch of undisturbed mud between the two."

"Intriguing," I remarked, "but that could be the shoe print of any woman who has walked along this pavement since yesterday."

"The imprint is rather fresh," replied my friend, taking a few steps forward towards the low wall. "Look at this other, older boot mark. The crest of mud around the pattern has been dried by the strong winds, while the hollow dent where the sole pushed down the mud has cupped some water from last night's rain."

"Still, this does not confirm that it belongs to Miss Harper."

The thought that Sherlock Holmes, brilliant as he was, could categorically ascribe the mudded imprint to a specific individual seemed ludicrous. I followed my companion back towards the steps. Once again, he bent down — adjusting the bottom of his coat — to indicate the fresher shoe print.

Holmes shook his head. "Look at the direction to which it points. The sole of the boot suggests the walker headed in a northeasterly direction from the southwest."

He turned round and gestured at the house. The two policemen, still standing idly by the entrance, looked perplexed.

"Someone came out of the house, down the steps and steered their course into the street. The only two women who could have done that since this morning were Miss Tilcott, the housemaid, and Miss Harper herself. Now the markings here are all characteristic of an expensive pair of boots. A housemaid's shoe heel would leave a larger impression than the one here. This boot was made for a sophisticated woman with money to spend."

Holmes rose up and sighed.

"Well, now that we have a rather firm grasp of the obvious, let us forge our own course towards Sekforde Street."

As we made it past Farringdon Lane the sickly glimmering lights floated just a few feet above our heads. On our way to Lucy Ward's lodgings, we passed a disgruntled Inspector

Lestrade, who had been conducting an extensive search of the southern end of the lane which intersected with Clerkenwell Green. He had ordered several constables to filter out into every street and form a wide ring round the site of the discovery of Miss Harper's hat.

Up until that moment, her whereabouts had remained elusive.

Before leaving the Inspector to his grumbling antics, complaining about a lack of resources and the untameable weather, Holmes took the hat from him and proceeded to examine it intensely. The scarlet bow was smudged, and the fabric of the bonnet severely trampled on by someone's aggressive footstep. It was a worrying sign and a desperate gambit against time.

Holmes barely spoke during the whole exchange with Lestrade. His eyes pierced the tiny details as he ran his fingers through the fine texture, remarking only how the bonnet was wet when there had been no rain since the night before.

"What is the meaning of this then, Mr. Holmes?" enquired the perplexed Scotland Yard official, as we left him and walked off to our destination.

"All in good time Inspector," cried my companion, glancing back over his shoulder.

"Is it Miss Harper's bonnet? Have you found out anything which could assist us?" I asked my companion.

"Perhaps," he said, "but I perceive, for good or ill, that we are soon on the threshold of finding out the whole truth."

Holmes raised the collar of his coat, dipped his hands into its pockets and paced in silent thought through the evening darkness.

His lack of conversation during our journey, affirmed my fears that Miss Eleonora Harper had indeed been kidnapped.

Chapter 8
A Knife in the Darkness

By now, the wind had picked up strength once again, and Sekforde Street looked even more uninviting than before.

A handful of pedestrians hurried on their way, leaving the road enveloped in an eerie silence. Our footsteps echoed with each dull thud on the stone pavement, as we reached the foreboding lodgings of Lucy Ward. The facade of the house, as identical in appearance as the ones adjacent to it, loomed in front of us with its daunting windows concealing within a gruesome mystery. Light emerged from one of these, presumably the landlady's own apartment.

"What now Holmes?" I asked, as we stood upon the doorstep. The appalling prospect of having to go back inside weighed heavily on my mind, and I was eager — even willing — to haunt some secluded alley or squalid London corner in pursuit of the investigation, rather than to venture once again through those tenebrous rooms.

Holmes moved away from the door and crouched low to the ground.

"We know from our friend Ruddy Wallace, that Miss Ward was seen in the company of a man late last night. We have identified that stranger as being Otto Becker from the imports warehouse, and who has now been categorically excluded from our inquiries." As he spoke, he repeated his earlier routine outside our client's house to check for any telling evidence.

What he hoped to see or find in that gloom was beyond my comprehension. There was no hope of discovering any imprint or any further clues after the heavy downpour of the previous night; not to mention the interminable flow of police officers in and out of Miss Ward's apartment — including our own that morning.

Yet Holmes persisted with his search with the aid of his lens. He scoured the tangle of shrubs that flanked the narrow path from the street to the door. All the while I heard him sniffing at regular intervals and suspected he had caught a nasty cold from Inspector Lestrade.

"Now all that remains is the piecing together of what must have occurred between Mr. Becker's departure from this place and our discovery of the body."

"As well as the murder weapon," I remarked.

"Quite right," Holmes panted. He was out of breath from leaning over the hedge, getting tangled in the bramble and pierced by prickly thorns.

"Halloa! What have we got here?" he suddenly exclaimed, rummaging through the twigs and leaves.

"An imprint? Another fingernail?" I gasped, running to his side.

"Neither." He pulled himself back up with much difficulty, and amid deep exhalation. In his hand he held the remains of a burnt cigar.

"Trichinopoly," he said, as he took another sniff at it as if to reaffirm his conclusions.

"How on earth did you find it?"

"I was looking for it. The scent is of a particular blend and was instantly perceptible as we ascended the steps just now."

"Do you think it is relevant?"

Holmes declined to answer but instead walked back out into the road. He stood under the light of a street lamp a few yards away, examining the charred cigar. I followed eagerly and paused beside him, waiting — feeling somewhat relieved at having distanced ourselves from the house.

"There's someone across the street looking right at us," said my friend on a sudden. He kept the cigar stub in front of his face while he spoke under his breath. I strained to look in the direction Holmes indicated, without being too obvious.

On the other side of the road, partly concealed within the shadows that lingered between each street lamp, stood a solitary figure. It was difficult to make out a face or even the overall appearance of the person, but a vague silhouette of someone staring at us was unmistakable. A few wisps of smoke emerged from a tiny glowing ember placed near its mouth.

"What do we do, Holmes? Who on earth could that be?" I whispered, trying to avoid making any sudden movements.

"Why don't we find out?" said Holmes, suddenly rushing forward across the street with a sprint.

The figure scurried away in the darkness and fled round the corner into Woodbridge Street, but Holmes's sure-footed dash was enough to keep him close behind the stranger.

I followed as fast as I could, but the chase came to an abrupt end when our runaway slid on the wet cobblestones and lost his balance, falling with a loud thud and a curse onto the ground. Holmes was on him in an instant, while I arrived shortly after, breathing hard and rubbing my strained leg.

"Mr. Phineas, I surmise," said Sherlock Holmes, gripping him under his arms and assisting him to sit up on the pavement. The man winced in pain and grumbled loudly, while tugging ferociously at my companion's grasp.

"Phineas Hunter the name be," came a gruff and threatening voice. "You best a-fear it once you've 'eard it."

The man pulled himself free from Holmes and sat on the cold, slippery stones of the pavement. He leered at us with deep, reddened eyes. Strands of lank hair fell over his contorted face — the skin was akin to the texture of a melted candle and punctured with scars of some past disease. Over his thin, pale mouth hung a mangled nose from which protruded thick dark hairs, as if to complement the knotted eyebrows under his forehead.

I looked closer and recalled his appearance: the mud stains on the black trousers, the long unkempt hair and the beaten top hat. All were discernible in the weak light.

"You're him," I said stepping forward, "You're the man I saw speaking to Mr. Wallace this afternoon." Holmes glanced at me in surprise.

"That decrepit Ruddy 'ain't got no sense in him," said Hunter, spitting phlegm on the ground. "What business is it of yours, leastways?"

"I believe this belongs to you," said Holmes, producing the charred cigar fragment.

"Bunkum! Never saw such thing. Now be off and leave us alone!"

"Certainly," retorted my friend. "But do not forget this," he added, picking up a freshly-extinguished cigar that had fallen from the man's grasp when he slipped.

"Gammon and spinach!" cried Hunter, raising himself resignedly in front of us.

"Who be you both eh?" he added, snatching the half-burnt cigar and relighting it with a broken match dug out from his trouser pocket.

The strong smell of the Trichinopoly blend was evident now even to me, as the man stood sneering from behind an endless stream of smoke.

"What is your interest in Lucy Ward?" asked my companion.

"And who be that?" said Hunter, taking another draw from his cigar.

"We know about the favours you asked of her and now she is dead. We are working with the police."

"Mutton shunters! Gah!" he spat once again and, as if disgusted by the words themselves, threw the cigar away.

"Mr. Hunter, if you know something which could assist us, then I strongly suggest you speak up. Otherwise, I see you as our main suspect." Holmes straightened himself up, stepping closer to the man who, despite his aggressive attitude, shrank back.

"Hornswoggle! What suspect? Me 'aint had nothin' to do with her, Miss Lu, as I called 'er. Just the odd bit 'o nanty narking, you know," he rambled. "As you says, a few *favours* for some coin." He gave off a cackle, almost animalistic, as if recalling past pleasures he had paid for. The conversation was unsettling and his behaviour loathsome.

"I sees the coppers this morning a-walkin' in an' out o' the house. They says nothing what happened and leaves the place as quick as they arrives. But cunnin' old Hunter knew the tale," he sneered, and tapped the side of his head with a long, claw-like fingernail. As he raised his hand, the sleeve of his coat fell down to reveal a small tainted tattoo just under the wrist. In the dark it presented itself as a series of letters or words. The ink was far from fresh but the mark was distinctive.

"Still," he said, "I thought I had to 'ave a look and make sure it was her. Ruddy told me about that German gal-sneaker she was a-with. Had to make sure just now when I sees the lights in the window. Then you two come all along, sneaks," he scoffed.

"Curious markings. What do they say?" said my friend, ignoring the remark and pointing at the tattoo. Hunter appeared hesitant and threatening, growling like a hunted dog, but he was soon at the mercy of Holmes who forcibly pulled up his hand and uncovered the words.

Divi filius.

" 'The son of a god'," uttered Holmes as he looked closer at the letters. "If I remember aright, most famously adopted by Emperor Augustus in that barbaric period of Ancient Rome — rather the epitome of narcissism and power, don't you think?" His last remark was given in my direction, as he looked at me with a stern expression on his face.

"A gang of sorts?" I asked, lowering my voice. Holmes nodded gently.

"It is a common occurrence for members of some organisations to brand themselves as a sign of allegiance to their leader," he whispered, "and it seems we may have a first name to those initials — *A. S.* — Augustus perhaps?"

The potential revelation was heartening. After so many ill-turns in our investigation we finally had something on which to work, scanty as it may have been.

"Oh aye, that's 'im alright," growled Hunter, as he inserted another lit cigar into his mouth. " 'The August Storm' me and the other lads would call 'im. And beware whoever stood in 'is way. I saw the sense in that not long after and abandoned that halfwit company. Too nasty for me taste." He puffed and sniggered at his own vile thoughts.

"Where can we find this man? Speak!" Holmes pressed the man for an answer.

Hunter's hoarse laugh was mixed with disgust. "Nargh! You don't get to 'im, *he* gets to *you*. But if you wants to meet 'im so eagerly," he added, with a sense of fear and fervour on his face, "there's a creaky old shed by the Old Brewery chimney, not far from 'ere. We used to meet a-there."

The man refused to reveal anything else, and no further threats of prison from my friend broke his staunch resolve.

The meeting place of the gang mentioned by Phineas Hunter, was an abandoned beerhouse a few corners away from Miss Ward's lodgings.

Having left the unsavoury Hunter behind us, with reassurance from Holmes that he would inform Inspector Lestrade about him, I followed my friend's sure and hurried steps along the winding streets, with the biting chill of evening to keep us company. A few minutes' walk led us round a bend into the aptly-named Brewhouse Yard, where the street opened up into a wide space occupied by several barns and brick buildings fenced off by a decaying wall bereft of a gate.

All signs of life seemed to end there at the entrance.

The light from the street lamps failed altogether as we plunged into complete darkness, making our way towards the tall structures that loomed up ahead. The brewery's chimney soared above the rest of the beerhouse, with its crown enmeshed in blackness.

Besides the crunching sounds of our shoes hitting the gravel, the silence around us was overpowering. I followed Holmes by his soft breathing and the heavy tread of his steps.

From within the enclosure, it was difficult to understand how the brewery was structured. Dim shapes appeared vaguely before us as we strained to pierce the shadows on our treacherous way towards the chimney. Both Holmes and I often found ourselves stumbling into some shallow pit, or a pile of broken wooden planks abandoned along our route.

As encouraging as our discovery of a potential name had been, the dreary investigation which had brought us to that place soon became even more austere. It was cold and damp, and the strong winds pushing down from the river dried my eyes and stung my skin. In those bleak, dark moments, I longed for the warm comfort of 221B, but the constant concern for our client's whereabouts and safety, hardened my will to see this through.

So I plodded on with what strength I had left, until my left foot stepped onto some unseen sludge and I slid forward.

"This accursed night will bring us no good," I grumbled, steadying myself just in time to maintain some balance.

"Hush Watson!" said Holmes. I could vaguely discern his broad shoulders in front of me crouching to the ground.

"What is it?" I whispered .

"A light over there," he said. Whether or not he had pointed at what he saw, I could not be certain. However, as we moved closer under what must have been the main building, a luminous point appeared in some hatch or window a few stories higher up. The light was weak, but it aided us in orienting ourselves in the darkness.

"Come! We must be discreet," came my friend's hoarse voice.

I stumbled forward as quietly as I could and before long was aware of some other radiance which shone ahead of us. A yellow glow seemed to intensify as it reflected off the grimy brick walls which we were now brushing against on our way to the chimney.

As my eyes adjusted to the faint light, the layout of the beerhouse became less dim. Glancing back, I could see the entrance and the low wall from which we had come, as well as the shed at the bottom of the chimney where we were cautiously making for.

Sherlock Holmes's silhouette darted across the last few yards, dangerously revealing himself to this other light which streamed out of some half-opened door in the main building.

He had done so with agility and without effort. I followed behind, slower and making a great deal of noise as I stamped on the coarse gravel. My heart was beating erratically, both from the physical exertion and the fear of being discovered.

By then we had reached the base of the chimney, with its dusty and charred stonework. I crouched beside Holmes, who strained his neck forward to get a glimpse of the open door which now stood on our right across what appeared to be a lawn.

We were concealed by the shadows and could now clearly see the facade of the building from which the light emerged.

As my heavy breathing relented, and the silence in my head settled once more, I was aware of voices coming from behind the door. A loud conversation between several men seemed to be taking place within the brewery itself. It was difficult to comprehend what was being said, but it was rather clear that an argument of sorts had broken out.

"This is it Watson," whispered Holmes eagerly, "the heart of the mystery. Still, I fear we may be outnumbered for the time being unless ..." he added with an impish tone to his voice, "... unless you care to knock and ask for the culprit to step forth."

"So what do we do now?" I asked, ignoring the remark.

"The murder weapon, Watson. If our criminal is this Augustus man, then this is the primary spot where we must commence our search."

I confess to the reader that by now the cold had started to seep deep into my bones. I was anxious, hungry, and exhausted from the day's events. The last thing I felt like doing was to pry around some violent gang's whereabouts. I sighed and shifted uneasily in my crouched position. Doubt gnawed my mind as I tried to piece together the events of that morning and the night before.

Holmes seemed to perceive my hesitation.

"What is it, Doctor?" he muttered.

"Well, it all seems unfounded. A worthless waste of time with no possible connection to the murder," I argued rather half-heartedly.

"Yet it is, after all, not too distant from Miss Ward's lodgings," said Holmes. "The coincidence is too significant for an oversight. Come!"

Before I could offer any more resistance, he stomped off from our hiding place. We stalked round the foot of the chimney and slid back into deep shadows, concealed from the line of sight of the threatening door.

"This is rather useless," I protested once again. "It will be impossible to search for clues in this dreadful darkness. We must come back in the morning."

"A moment, Watson, pray!" exclaimed Holmes in a hoarse whisper.

He crouched there, resting his right hand against the brickwork whilst looking towards the path we had come from. For several minutes he remained motionless without saying a word.

"Yesterday's rain will have seeped into the ground by now," he said suddenly. "Undoubtedly, the murderer left Miss Ward's lodgings during the storm. Any trace of blood on the weapon or his clothes will have been almost completely washed away. There was no blood in Miss Ward's room either, except for the bed itself — a significant point. So ..."

Here he paused momentarily as if to collect his thoughts before he began once again to state his point. "If our man made his way here last night to discard the murder weapon, he must have concealed it in something, some kind of cloth, to avoid any bloodstains in the apartment. He would then have had to follow the same route and path that we have done just now, while carrying the bundle with him — at least up until that door itself." He pointed at the doorway from which the light shone.

"Why not dispose of the weapon beforehand? Why come all the way to leave it here?" I argued, feeling the impossibility of my friend's statement become even more far-fetched.

"If we are to go by Mr. Hunter's claim, and I dare say he was not too far from the truth," said Holmes, keeping his eyes fixed on the doorway from which the voices emerged, "this is Augustus's hiding place. One would instinctively resort to seeking refuge in a trusted place, especially after such a criminal act."

He cupped some gravel and dirt in his hands, rubbing them gently between his palms and fingers. In the murky shadows, it seemed soft and pulpy.

"The incessant rain would have weakened the surface of this whole area," he continued, "while inevitably forcing our culprit to make a dash for the building, leaving deep imprints in the ground. Remember the boot markings by Miss Harper's house? The same logic applies here. Since then, the rain will have filled the boot prints with water, but the edges of the impressions formed by each foot would have remained there, only to dry and solidify with the drying effect of the strong wind. Might it be possible?" he asked, as if debating with himself. "Yes, perhaps ... perhaps we could still trace those prints now. Come," he said, glancing at me, "let us inspect the ground and hope to substantiate our hypothesis!"

With that remark, he rushed out again onto the main path, right in sight of the door.

I rose to my feet, gazing at a hunched Holmes surveying the ground in the threatening light. My heart began to tremble even faster than before, as excitement fuelled my mind and dispelled any accumulated weariness. Raising myself up, I took a deep breath and hurried towards my companion, trying to make as little noise as possible.

I reached Holmes as he lowered himself on one knee, bending down towards the ground, making use of the light that streamed out in order to assist in his investigation. Alarmingly, we were directly in front of the open door and the voices had grown significantly louder. I could vaguely discern a long corridor plunging deep into the building; other than that, there was nothing else I could see.

"Watson, look!" said Holmes sharply.

He was pointing at a disturbed patch of earth a few yards away from the doorstep. I bent down for closer observation, but a loud thud forced me to look up again at the menace inside. From the babble of voices, it appeared that the ensuing argument between the strangers in the building had erupted into a scuffle.

"Watson, the imprint!" came Holmes's voice, urging me to focus on his discovery.

There was a clear outline of a depression in the ground, in the form of a sharply curved crescent moon. The impression was deep and a little water lay at its base. Upon further inspection, I realised there was no sign of a heel mark to accompany it. Holmes's hypothesis that the man had run across the path towards the building seemed viable.

"There are a few more, further back here," whispered Holmes, having taken a few steps away from me. "And they all seem to point over there," he added, raising his hand towards me. The voices inside the building grew louder and heavy footsteps could be heard echoing along the corridor.

"Holmes!" I cried hoarsely.

My friend, momentarily distracted by these findings, looked up at the building and came forward.

"Not a minute to lose Doctor, now for it!" He ran past me, leaving the path and heading towards a shed which lay between the brick building and the chimney.

We hid once more in the shadows and watched the entrance to the door as two burly men came out. They paused close by where we had discovered the footprint and stood arguing. Their voices, filling the crisp air, were loud and harsh. One of them seemed to turn round to face the door while shouting a few other incomprehensible words. Other occupants, besides those two, seemed to be lingering inside.

I was peering from behind a stack of crates left under the cracked roof of the shed. In that gloom, it presented itself as a decrepit wooden structure on the point of collapse. As the strong wind howled, the wooden posts that held the whole thing together, creaked ominously. The shack, which still smelt of malt and yeast, was open at the front, as the doors that had once hung there seemed to have long since disappeared.

Holmes was crouched behind me, further back in the darkness. He made a good deal of noise as he seemed to be crawling along the ground. I, however, kept my eyes on the two men outside, hoping they would leave the brewery. The argument was becoming more fierce as arms were waved wildly and several shouts added to the fray. Suddenly, as I knelt there, concealed in the safety of the shed, a glow of light illuminated the dilapidated crates I was hiding behind.

Momentarily struck by this odd occurrence and the odour of burning oil, I turned round to find Holmes fiddling with a battered lantern he seemed to have found. A bright radiance sprang forth, lighting up a substantial part of the shed.

"Holmes! What the devil are you doing?"

I looked back in alarm at the main building where the men stood. There was no reason to believe they had seen the light, but my initial sense of excitement at our pursuit suddenly turned into one of dread. I was sure that Holmes's blunder would lead to our discovery and bring terrible peril.

"Put that light out!" I implored, trying to keep my voice down.

The consulting detective, who on many occasions I have praised as being one of the wisest and best men I have known, ignored my distress and raised the lantern high above his head. He was bowed down, facing one of the corners of the shed, while his other hand sifted through some empty sacks. Abandoning my vigil by the crates, I crawled towards him and looked over his shoulder.

In his hand he held a blood-stained bundle of cloth. Placing the lantern on one of the crates, he undid the fabric which turned out to be a shirt with long sleeves. Inside lay a short, sharp-edged knife with a dark blood-stained wooden handle.

"I have read the clues aright," said Holmes, carefully removing the weapon. "This is the decisive link in our chain, Watson." He raised the knife as if to emphasise his statement.

"And what is that?" I said, leaning closer to point at a tiny piece of string which stuck loosely between the blade and the handle. Holmes brought the knife closer to the lantern and removed the strand with his fingers. He used his magnifying lens to inspect in detail the string he held before him.

"It is a piece of fabric. Very peculiar I must say," he said after a while. "It seems to come from some kind of uniform," he concluded with some hesitation.

The statement struck me as odd, but as I crawled forward to reach out for the strand and come up with my own conclusions, my shoulder brushed against the lantern on the crate and knocked it over with a loud crash.

In a single, tremulous heartbeat, I instinctively turned round to face a dreadful sight.

The voices from outside were coming towards us, along with several hurried footsteps.

"Holmes! We have been discovered!"

My companion hastily tucked the knife back in the bundle and raised himself up.

"Time to run Watson!"

Chapter 9
Holmes Sets a Trap

"Quick Watson! Through here!"

Holmes's firm voice was followed by a loud crash coming from the back of the barn. Crouching deep in the shadows behind my friend, I scurried on both hands and knees through a large crack in the wall of the shed. My friend had forced a rift through the weak wall as a means of escape.

The hoarse cries from outside came closer, and the thud of heavy footsteps had reached the entrance of the barn by the time I emerged from behind the brittle structure.

It was dark, cold and wet, and my head was thumping fiercely. I lost all sense of direction but was spurred on by Holmes's sharp cry as he urged me to follow him round the back of the main brewery building.

I staggered to my feet, stumbling in the darkness, while following as quick as my legs could carry me. A few paces ahead, I could hear the furtive steps of my friend's boots crunching the rough gravel.

The voices behind grew faint, but a violent uproar signalled the arrival of more men, as the search intensified. It was only a matter of seconds before the breach in the barn would be discovered and the direction of our escape made known.

The blackness was almost complete. Vague shapes and gloomy shadows were of little help as I ran as fast as I could, while the crisp air brushed mercilessly against my face, stinging my eyes.

There was no light coming through the windows on this side of the building, which, although helping to conceal our desperate flight also hindered our path.

I was gasping furiously and my muscles ached with this sudden burst of energy. However, fear numbed all pain and gave me enough strength to push myself forward.

A sudden, abrupt movement from Holmes ahead warned me that we had reached the far side of the brewery, and that he had made a dash round the corner. As I shifted my balance to follow him without slowing down my pace, I discerned lights at the corner of my eye. Glancing backwards I saw several men carrying lanterns rushing through the breach and running in our direction.

I steadied myself against the rotten brick wall and dashed forward.

"Watson!" cried Holmes just ahead.

The darkness was now less deep as we came back to the front side of the brewery. We were crossing the open ground and making for the main entrance of the outer fence, when my left foot caught in a pile of wood, sending me crashing to the ground. I gasped loudly as the air was driven out of my lungs by the violent impact. Before the agony of the fall set in, I crawled forward in terror as the heavy footsteps and harsh voices came nearer. I looked back once more in desperation, noticing the intensifying glow that signalled the imminent approach of our pursuers.

Crawling slowly forward, I was suddenly hauled up by powerful arms and set on my feet. I felt the small pieces of coarse gravel falling off my coat and trousers, while a tightness gripped my chest.

"All in one piece Watson," said Holmes breathlessly. "Now for it!"

He was off again as soon as he said those words, while I followed as best I could. The sharp spasms from the fall weakened my sprint, but the sight of the men just a few yards behind was enough to keep me going just a little further.

We reached the opening of the fence with the missing gate in Brewhouse Yard and plunged into a narrow side alley a few yards along the street. Holmes and I squeezed ourselves behind a few boxes piled on top of each other, breathing heavily in the silent darkness. As we peered through the crevices between the boxes, we could discern the path of the street we had just abandoned. The clamour of voices and rush of footsteps grew louder, until the gang came closer. Several men, clad in ragged clothes, bearing lanterns and knives, dashed past our place of concealment and scattered through the widening streets ahead.

"What say you if we seek the comfort of 221B?" whispered Holmes as soon as the uproar had receded.

The suggestion was greatly welcomed and I sighed and nodded with sincere approval and resolve.

"Shouldn't we let Inspector Lestrade know, now that we have found out about the gang's meeting place?"

Holmes shook his head. "Whether or not this Augustus was present here, I would still not risk alarming him with Scotland Yard's officers, and allowing all this to become a fruitless chase."

Nevertheless, it was a long and trying time until we eventually retraced our steps back to Baker Street.

With the hunt still on, we could not risk being discovered. It made no difference whether or not our faces had been recognised at the brewery. Two men running furtively along the streets at night was enough to raise suspicion. We therefore made our slow and cautious way back to familiar quarters. The gang may have been keeping an eye on numerous roads and areas, but Holmes's superior knowledge of London's labyrinthine streets was no match for the minds of scroungers and criminals that stalked the City's walkways.

It was thus close to midnight when we stumbled wearily into our lodgings.

Holmes relit the fire to warm up the sitting-room and slipped into his dressing gown, with his briar pipe in hand.

"I suggest you take some rest Doctor," he said, settling down in his armchair. "Tomorrow's need will be greater."

Without a word, I staggered to my bedroom, leaving Holmes to his pipe-smoke and thinking.

The soft caress of the pillow, as I laid my throbbing head on it, sent me swiftly into a deep sleep.

My repose was abruptly disturbed the following morning, as I was woken by a thunderous noise. It sounded like an avalanche that had swept into the sitting-room, leaving my heart fluttering wildly and my head spinning. I rose unsteadily from the bed, my body stiff and still aching from the previous night's predicament.

Dizzy and exhausted, I made my way to the sitting-room, where the clamour increased with every step.

As I walked in, Sherlock Holmes was bending low on the floor beside the sofa. It had been pushed aside abruptly and had, as a result, knocked over the small table by the door. The carpet was rumpled by the displaced furniture, while my friend crawled further down towards the far corner.

The air in the room was stuffy and smelt strongly of burnt tobacco.

"Just a moment Doctor," came Holmes's muffled and breathless voice. He eventually raised himself up to his knees and turned round. By the odour of the smoke and the distinct rings round my friend's eyes, it was evident that he had stayed up all night.

"What on earth are you doing?" I protested in annoyance.

"Apologies Watson. I was undertaking an investigation," he replied with a smirk.

"In the sitting-room?" I retorted in disbelief.

He stood up and came towards me, his bare feet brushing against the carpet.

"What do you see?" he asked quietly. He raised his right hand before me, holding a pair of small pincers with his fingers. The dizziness had not fully passed, and I struggled to comprehend my friend's odd request.

Upon closer inspection, I noticed a small fragment held tight between the two metal jaws. As the haze before my eyes lessened, there was no doubt about what I saw.

A jagged piece of fingernail was held in the grip of that tool.

Between the drowsiness and the fright of the noise, I failed to make out any meaning of it.

"One of yours?" I asked. "Or perhaps mine?" I added, looking meekly at my hands.

"Neither," said Holmes. He took another step closer towards me.

"Discovered just this morning by the sofa. What say you to that?" He held the pincers behind his magnifying glass to enlarge the details of the fragment. The yellow-stained piece seemed to be broken, and vaguely reminiscent of the two other pieces of nail we had found the previous day.

The thought struck me in an instant.

The finding of that piece of nail in our lodgings was too coincidental and meant only one thing.

"You don't suppose …?" I began.

"That is precisely what I think."

"But how …?"

"It would seem our murderer is closer to us than we may realise."

My head spinning with agitation and bewilderment, I staggered forward and collapsed into one of the armchairs.

"I found it shortly after dawn, during one of my intense reflections," said Holmes. "I had been pondering over the details of yesterday's events, while clearing my head with a new blend of tobacco, when I glimpsed that piece of nail upon the carpet."

A chill ran down my spine and the palms of my hands became damp with sweat.

"I am sorry to cascade all of this upon you so early in the morning," said my companion, as he placed the pincers upon the mantlepiece and relit his pipe. "It would seem that the riddles of this case are hurtling towards us. If I read the signs aright, before this day is over we shall be familiar with the truth — for good or ill."

"I don't understand," I stammered, rubbing my forehead to ease the headache that had so suddenly returned to afflict me.

"Perhaps this might help to clear your doubts," said Holmes suddenly, pointing at a tiny smear on one of the sofa's cushions.

Rising from the chair, I bent down to the floor. I had to squint my eyes to peer through Holmes's magnifying glass in order to focus on the dark stain. The mark was extremely small, and yet perceptible on the light colour of the cushion. It had been smudged into the fabric as if pressed upon with force. I leaned closer, adjusting the glass accordingly, only to realise a touch of scarlet in that black speck.

"Blood?"

Raising my head, I noticed the keen stare with which my friend looked at me. He nodded slowly, before taking another swift draw from his pipe.

I recalled the events of the day before: the gruesome murder of Lucy Ward, the German stranger, Inspector Lestrade's news of our client's disappearance …

As these thoughts raced through my head, my gaze landed on the knife we had found at the old brewery. It lay there upon the mantelpiece, with the tiny strand of fabric still stuck, between the blade and the handle.

"The uniform!" I exclaimed. Inspector Lestrade's warning to his constables in that same sitting-room flooded my mind, but only one had recoiled from the Inspector's threats, brushing against the sofa.

"Holmes ..."

My friend raised his hand as if to interrupt my statement.

"Let us not twist facts to suit theories, Watson. Rather, let us twist theories to suit facts," he said, standing up. He abandoned the pipe on the armchair and stood beside me, speaking softly in my ear.

"Now, I need your assistance for a little plan I have concocted," said Holmes, placing his hand gently on my shoulder. "Your service would be appreciated, but I need you in splendid form, Watson. Do you think you can see to that?"

"Absolutely," I proclaimed rather too eagerly. I looked in earnest at my companion.

"I take it you have not yet acquainted yourself with this morning's missing items section in *The Times*? I find it exquisitely instructive," he said abruptly, handing me a copy of the newspaper from the littered desk by the door.

I looked at it, confused — not knowing what I was looking for. I gazed back at Holmes who kept his eyes on the newspaper I held in my hands.

Shuffling through the coarse pages of the paper, I folded it, revealing the specified section. I glanced through the list, until my eyes were drawn towards a set of familiar words. The announcement in question ran in this way:

"Lost.— bonnet with scarlet bow near Farringdon Lane. The sum of five shillings will be paid to any one who can give information to Miss Eleonora Harper, at No. 11 Warner Street — 10 o'clock onwards."

I scrutinised the advertisement once again to reassure myself of what I had just read. The presence of the announcement in that morning's newspaper made no sense, and what all this really meant was far from comprehensible.

"So you know where Miss Harper is?" I gasped. "Is she safe?"

"All in good time Doctor," said Sherlock Holmes quietly. "Now off with these gowns. The game is afoot."

I knew there was no way of convincing my friend to divulge any of his plans prematurely. This news of Miss Harper's apparent well-being was heartening, but dubious.

Nevertheless, I too felt that we were coming to the end of this tangled case and was eager to see it resolved as promptly as could be arranged.

It was almost 9 o'clock when we made ready to embark on the second day of our case.

Without any clear indication of what Sherlock Holmes had in mind, or where our adventure would lead us, we emerged into Baker Street.

The bitter cold was persistent, and the grey clouds only gathered closer and thicker over London. By then, any promise of rain had in turn been replaced by a gentle snowfall that fell softly onto the streets, steadily coating the brown-hued appearance of the city with a white layer of fluffy flakes.

We accosted a cab and made our way to the nearest post office, as Holmes intended to dispatch a telegram. Soon after, we returned to the gentler bustle at Warner Street, alighting a few doors away from Miss Harper's house.

"This way Watson," said Holmes, as he led me to a narrow alley on the southern side of the street, running for a few yards before being blocked off by a high wall.

"Now what?" I asked.

"Now we wait."

The snow was descending steadily, but our position provided some shelter from the cold. We could not observe Warner Street itself, but occasionally Sherlock Holmes would peer out from the passage we were in and glance at the doors which led down towards Miss Harper's house. I allowed myself a brief glimpse, noticing the lonesome aspect of the road.

It must have been over half an hour, standing there watching and waiting. I pestered Holmes with questions, pressing him to reveal anything that could help alleviate the unbearable sense of being left in the dark.

"Ever since the beginning of this case," he sighed, peering once again into the street, "I found myself pondering on the difficulties of linking the disappearance of our client with the murderous act upon Miss Lucy Ward. The two occurrences were too striking to be a mere coincidence, and yet I felt that our culprit had nothing to do with the sudden disappearance of Eleonora Harper."

"How so?" I whispered, feeling the loose threads of the case beginning to intertwine.

"For one thing, the presence of the abandoned bonnet. As I held it in my hands, the report of it having been somehow lost in the midst of a scuffle — presumably in the attempt to seize Miss Harper — was in conflict with what my eyes saw."

Holmes paused for a moment as if recalling the details. He looked at my inquisitive expression and continued.

"The smudged boot imprint on the hat, Watson. The whole thing looked too contrived, too methodical. It was as if the hat were deliberately stepped upon and placed — rather than thrown — on the ground."

The argument proposed by my friend was quite unexpected, and yet I remembered how Holmes's silent expression during his analysis of the bonnet had struck me as odd.

"That fact alone reinforced my belief that there was indeed no kidnapping at all," he continued, "but given the news of her friend's murder, it seems Miss Harper decided to take matters into her own hands."

"Holmes, are you saying this disappearance is mere pretence?" I exclaimed.

"Consider Watson. You fear for your life after receiving a mysterious letter. Then, the morning after you visit a consulting detective, your friend is found brutally murdered in her apartment. Trust in the police force is not a viable option, and the only desperate way of avoiding a similar gruesome fate, is to abandon ship."

"So you have no news of Miss Harper's whereabouts then?"

"I'm afraid not Watson, but we can rest better knowing that in all probability she is safer than we previously thought she was."

"And what about our culprit? Is he still on the hunt for Miss Harper?"

"That is a strong supposition which we shall soon be able to support or refute."

Holmes peered once again out into the street, staring for several minutes — observing the solitary passersby strolling along that stretch of road. I joined my friend in the watch, straining my head and shoulders out of our concealment to get a favourable glimpse of the other end of the street. By then, the ground was caked in a fine blanket of snow, while the occasional gusts of wind blew a flurry of flakes in a dizzying spectacle.

"I therefore thought it the most suitable time," said Holmes from behind my back, "to attempt to lure the murderous rogue by placing that announcement in the newspaper, pretending to be Miss Harper — dismissing any rumours of her disappearance — and enticing the culprit back to our client's house. Whatever this villain has against our client, it must be personal and he will not risk sending any other of his men to see to the task. The same thought no doubt ran through his head when he decided to act upon the poor Lucy Ward. There was cunning skill and violence in those wounds, Watson. Whoever Augustus is, his mind and physical strength reach beyond the prowess of that handful of scoundrels he rules over."

"Ingenious, Holmes," I winced, as my eyes attempted to pierce through the increasing haze of snow which had begun to envelope the street. "But how can we be sure he has seen the newspaper advertisement at all?"

"That is why we wait," he replied.

He resumed his watch, patiently observing every subtle movement or change in the street.

As our conversation came to an end, the silence returned. The faint rumble of busier quarters close by echoed along the road, accompanied by the wind hissing in our ears. I abandoned my lookout and joined Holmes in his inspection of Miss Harper's house.

The front steps were still in sight, but the snowfall had reduced the visibility.

Holmes sighed, mumbling something incoherent.

"How about a brief walk?" he said promptly. He straightened his coat and emerged into the street with his hands behind his back.

"Now?" I asked, as I followed him bewildered by the unexpected suggestion. "What about the house? What if the murderer comes while we're away?"

"That has already been seen to. I have my informant inside," he said with a slight grin.

"Who?"

"It's Miss Tilcott, the housemaid," said Holmes, lowering his voice. "It was to her that I sent this morning's telegram. I've asked her not to answer the door today, but report back to me should anything amiss occur."

Reluctant as I was at leaving the house unguarded, with additional misgivings at having abandoned that sheltered alley, I raised the collar of my coat as we made our way in silence towards St. James's Church Garden — that same tranquil place I had ventured into the previous day, in my fruitless search for Eleonora Harper. As we turned sharply into the church courtyard, a man came running out — crashing into my left side and knocking me over. It was a powerful jolt, but the pain of the initial impact soon subsided.

The man was gone in an instant, his hasty footsteps receding far back up the street from where we had come. I was hoisted back up by Holmes, who had shouted at the individual in an attempt to make him stop. Momentarily distracted by the annoyance of what had just happened, my mind felt easier as we continued on our way.

The scene that greeted us when we arrived at the church was serene, but the bright green sward had by then been covered with snow. We headed round the church on the eastern side when Holmes suddenly stretched out his hand in front of me. We halted under a withering elm tree drooping heavily over the church's outlying porch.

There, on the ground, the snow had been disturbed by some great commotion. It had been scooped up and brushed away with considerable force, with tufts of grass plucked out of the ground. Besides the tainted ivory colour of the silt, there were smears of faint crimson stains upon the snow.

Sherlock Holmes bent down and ran his hand through the supple flakes, letting their texture slide through his fingers. He glanced ahead towards the side of the church and took a few steps forward. As he did, several grunts and agonised breathing escaped from the mouth of a man lying twisted under the ledge of a window. As we drew closer, Phineas Hunter's distinct appearance revealed itself to us.

His hat was gone and he bore a pained expression on his pale face. Blood trickled from his mouth and nose, while he clutched the right side of his ribcage.

We ran towards the ailing man on the ground. Upon closer inspection, deep cuts and contusions were visible across his face and hands, as if he had been violently kicked and beaten.

Holmes opened the man's shirt collar as he gasped for air.

"Mr. Hunter, who did this to you?" he demanded, grabbing hold of the other's hands as he waved them in front of his face.

"Revenge!" he gasped, "Augustus's wrath … revenge!"

He repeated the phrase over and over, all the while as his voice grew more faint.

"Watson come! We must see to Miss Tilcott this instant," cried Holmes, leaping to his feet and dashing across the sward into the street.

My mind recalled the man who had knocked me over just then, and the direction in which he was headed. Holmes was already making his way out of the courtyard. Yet, compelled by my sense of duty as a doctor, I lingered a while longer.

Instinctively, I took off my coat to cover Phineas Hunter with it, making sure he was conscious, while carefully raising his head to rest upon my scarf which acted as a pillow.

I gave a reassuring pat to the patient and rose to my feet to follow Holmes.

Just at that moment, a heavy blow smote me on the head and everything went dark.

Chapter 10
Footsteps in the Snow

The blackness began to recede, slowly at first, then gradually as I regained consciousness.

I felt weak and unable to open my eyes as my facial muscles were tense and ached from the strain. A frosted speck slid gently down the side of my left cheek. I could sense the tiny particle's cold trail upon my skin, sending a persistent chill which spread from my head down to my lower back.

I convinced myself that I was still alive and just feeling nauseous — which was oddly reassuring. Some strength returned to my arms, allowing me to move them gently, as coarse snow slithered through my fingers. The cold caress of the ground beneath me intensified, and for a moment I could only hear the muffled cacophony of turmoil around me, as I lay in some nightmare from which I could not wake up.

With some exertion, I raised my eyelids to witness a blurred haze of snowflakes falling on me. The sky was a puddle of grey, and beneath it the whitened tips of elm trees swayed in some imperceptible breeze. I raised my head to look further down and a sharp pain throbbed fiercely round the back of my skull. I felt sick and the agony flooded my mind with glimpses from moments earlier.

I recalled Holmes and myself venturing into the church courtyard, only to discover the wounded Phineas Hunter. My companion had suddenly dashed away from the scene, but a powerful blow from behind had soon after knocked me over.

I now bore a severe headache and my body shook from the cold and the crushing pain. Forcing myself to sit upright, I wanted to find out what the source of the unrelenting tumult was.

Fighting off the urge to wince at every slight movement I made, the haze before my eyes cleared enough for me to see two figures locked in each other's grip, one struggling to overthrow the other. They were a few yards ahead, towards the entrance to the courtyard. Like some brutal dance, they released each other and swiftly took a step back. The one on the left held some kind of knife as his outstretched arm was pointing aggressively at his opponent, who in turn seemed to maintain a calm and composed disposition.

As the flurry persisted, the two men charged once more, sending clouds of disturbed snow flying all around them with the vigorous stomping of their shoes. Grunts ensued as the man with the knife lunged forward, struggling once again to skewer his foe. The attempts were fruitless as the other evaded each thrust with relative ease, before he himself brought his right arm crashing down onto the knife, forcing it to fall to the ground. Without halting, he brought himself in between the man's outstretched arm and drove his elbow into the assailant's chest, sending him toppling onto the snow with an agonising cry.

I watched behind the intensifying veil of pattering flakes as the winner of the duel bent down to pick up the knife, before rushing forward in my direction.

Sudden dread numbed the pain in my head, and an urge to run away to safety forced me to stagger onto my feet, before faltering backwards and steadying myself against one of the church's window ledges. A few paces away, an unconscious Phineas Hunter sat in the snow with his back propped against the stone wall.

The figure came towards me with swift steps through the piles of snow.

"Watson! Goodness, you're alive!" said a voice, which suspiciously reminded me of my companion. Indeed, Holmes's stern face emerged through the flurry as he came to help me stand up straight. Glancing at him momentarily, I caught a perceptible sense of relief in his clear eyes.

"One of Augustus's men," said Holmes, pointing to the ruffian he had knocked over. He produced a short, crooked blade with a cracked wooden pommel.

While relieved by Holmes's presence, seeing the damaged knife made me brush my hand against the back of my head, feeling the sore wound that might have been caused by that weapon's hilt. I rubbed my fingers together and held my hand up. There was no sign of blood.

"Come! We must go back to Miss Harper's house this instant," said Sherlock Holmes, stowing the knife in one of his coat pockets while retracing his steps back towards the entrance.

I followed as best I could, but the constant throbbing in my head and the weakness in my legs made it hard to follow the surefooted strides my friend took upon the snow-covered path.

As I emerged out of St. James's Church Green and into the street, I caught a glimpse of my friend running up Clerkenwell Close, before plunging into a side alley to his left. The discovery of the wounded Phineas Hunter and the thought of a dangerous man's gang close on our heels, held my strength and spirit together. Not to mention the innocent Miss Tilcott, unaware of her danger as she stood in the way of Augustus's inexplicable vengeance upon her mistress.

The thrill of the chase aided my pursuit and eased the pain I was in. I was able to run in short bursts, before slowing down to a brisk walk, gradually picking my way towards Warner Street.

By then, the snow was falling ceaselessly down onto the city. A swirling mist enveloped the streets and pedestrians wrapped their clothing tighter around them to keep the cold at bay.

By the time we had converged on Farringdon Road, and cut across into a narrow passage towards the eastern side of Warner Street, I was breathing heavily and the pounding in my head only got worse. As with the other streets, lamps and lanterns had been lit to aid passersby and the traffic that lumbered along the roadway, but most of their light had been swallowed up by the murky conditions.

"Stay Watson!" said Sherlock Holmes, as he paused a few doors down from Miss Harper's house — waiting for me to catch up. He held his outstretched hand in my direction, looking ahead as if attempting to pierce the veil before us.

"We are stepping into the trail of vicious criminals, and must exercise proper caution. Let us not fall victims to a similar attack as the savage one laid on you just moments ago. We do not want that," he said, taking a few cautious steps forward.

"*I* do not want that," he corrected himself, lowering his voice. He said these last words with some exertion, as his voice quivered ever so subtly.

It was an admiring trait of my friend's that, although unwilling to express his emotions as any other human being would, he was capable of concealing them with such vigorous and admirable determination. Yet, a gentle crack behind that stern face would reveal itself from time to time.

In that dismal weather and bitter circumstances, it lightened my heart to hear it. Suddenly, those kind words were soon interrupted by a loud crash and the piercing screams of a woman coming from further up the road.

"It's Miss Tilcott!" yelled Holmes, dashing ahead once again. His steps fell with a faint crunching sound on the snow, and within a few seconds he disappeared from my sight. I followed immediately, directing myself by the woman's cries, just managing to make out the shape of my friend as he climbed the stairs and plunged into Eleonora Harper's house through the front door, which appeared to have been forcibly opened.

Gruesome thoughts raced through my mind as I left the pavement and ascended the stairs. My will was upon the verge of faltering. Scenes from the bloodied body of Lucy Ward brought me to a halt on the last step. Those screams coming from inside, together with the constant pursuit of fears and dangers we faced throughout this case, forced me to conjure up some horrible fate that the young housemaid was being subjected to. As I stood by the door, which had been forced open by some savage kick or thrust to the handle, another scream came from inside.

Shaken from these heinous thoughts, I rushed into the house with an unsettled resolve.

The air inside was warm and mixed with a tinge of spices. Along the corridor were signs of a scuffle, with pieces of fabric and broken furniture strewn upon the floor. A trail of sludge and mudded footsteps led me to the parlour.

"Constable! Leave that woman alone!" roared the voice of my companion from within. The noise of shattering window panes and a loud thud cut off the woman's scream. I burst inside to find Miss Tilcott crouching beside a large sofa — shivering and crying with fear.

Shards of glass were scattered all around her, and I just managed to make out the intruder's police uniform running back out into the street.

"It's Clarke isn't?" I exclaimed breathlessly. The face of the imposing constable, whose timid character had shrunk away from a wrathful Lestrade in our own sitting-room came to mind.

Before he could answer, Sherlock Holmes's frame squeezed through the broken window in pursuit. I helped the housemaid onto the sofa and attempted to say a few encouraging words which, in the thrill of the hunt, I cannot now recall.

Leaving Miss Tilcott to recover, I headed back outside.

Holmes was already running down the street, taking a sharp right and disappearing into a narrow roadway in pursuit of his prey. Following my companion, I plunged into the relative calm and gloom of Eyre Street Hill — its cramped conditions providing for an ideal shelter from the snowfall. As we ran, the smell of roasting chestnuts rose eagerly into the air from several carts lined up along the pavement. Women in meagre clothing were huddled beside each other upon the doorsteps, looking up at us with strange silent faces. Warm air was trapped by the overhanging decrepit buildings as steam and white smoke emerged from concealed outlets.

The cobblestones in the road had become slippery from the snow and, as I looked up, a few paces ahead of Holmes with his coat flying behind him, the uniformed assailant slipped and tumbled forward onto his hands. He had arrived at the end of the road but swiftly staggered to his feet before disappearing once again into the misty veil.

Holmes and I had gained a few steps, taking a left turn towards the east when the street opened up before us.

We had left the silence behind and emerged once again into the cold and long bustling lanes of Clerkenwell Road. Here, the people of London had not shuddered away from the snowfall but seemed to gain renewed strength — rejoicing in the festive atmosphere that lay upon this part of the city. Our assailant flitted between the hundreds of pedestrians occupying the pavements as they scuttled in and out of buildings or were hindered by costermongers' wagons. Some stood around in huddled groups laughing and crying out in joyous stupor at the persistent snowflakes falling on their clothing and around them.

Yet, our pursuit continued.

Holmes, by some imperceptible skill or other, seemed to know which way to go. He darted among the people and on many occasions only narrowly avoided colliding violently with them.

The confusion and the noise in the street made me dizzy and the throbbing pain at the back of my head returned. I fell behind and could not hope to catch up with my friend's quick steps. Clerkenwell Road stretched for over half a mile and, as we raced along it, the whole chase felt interminable. I was out of breath and my legs ached. The thought of being so close to the resolution of the case and discovering the fate of Eleonora Harper had kept me going for a while, but eventually that strength began to dissipate.

Just at that moment, as I began to slow down into an exhausted walk, a shout rose above the tumult.

"Halloa! You boy!" cried Holmes suddenly. "Wiggins!"

He was a few yards away, pointing his finger at a familiar street Arab — a young man in dirty, ragged clothes — standing alone across the street at a corner. Upon hearing his name, he sharply drew back his hand from over a nearby fruit-filled cart.

The boy came running over to my companion, who spoke to him earnestly. I followed as swiftly as I could, and by the time I reached them, Holmes had hailed a cab and helped the boy inside — much to the concern of the driver, but whose anguished face turned to glee on receiving a handful of coins. The hansom turned sharply round and dashed off in the opposite direction from which we had come, bearing the principal member of the Baker Street Irregulars on some urgent errand.

"Come Watson! Our assailant is far ahead!" My companion waved his hand high above his head and shouted at another approaching cab. I was pulled inside while Holmes cried in a loud voice, "Brewhouse Yard! And not another moment to lose!" He sat down opposite me, straining his head out of the window as the cab rattled furiously down the road.

"Quite the hunt is it not!" he exclaimed, keeping his gaze fixed upon the fleeting world outside.

I had regained some strength in the warm and compact enclosure of the cab. With the commotion outside now shut out, my head was no longer spinning and the ache in my legs eased off a little.

"Why the brewery, Holmes?" I asked in a drowsy voice. He did not answer for a while, as his eyes were still staring far ahead hoping to keep his prey in sight.

"It is the meeting place of Augustus's gang and this road leads directly towards it," he said, pausing for a moment. He looked away from the window as if struck by a sudden thought, as if in doubt. He struggled to speak, until he finally picked up the conversation.

"I cannot be certain of course, but that seems to be the only likely possibility. Anyway, we shall soon find out — here is where we turn round into Aylesbury Street."

The driver roared above the thundering hooves, pulling at the reins of the horses as he swerved to the side, readjusting his route in a northerly direction.

"Did you know it was Clarke — Augustus I mean?" I said, rubbing my head gently.

"I had whittled down my suspicions of Augustus's identity to two possible individuals," said Holmes. "Our little advertisement on the newspaper worked wonderfully, were it not for his vicious attack on Phineas Hunter. Yet, it is the complete success of our trap that I am now beginning to fear that not even Augustus knows where Miss Harper really is. Why would he seek her out at her house, if he were responsible for kidnapping her in the first place?"

He paused for a while, looking again at the rushing doors and lamp posts on that narrow street.

"Inconsistent," he muttered to himself, rubbing his hand against his chiselled chin. "Clearly something else is afoot beside this quest of ours," he said, glancing furtively in my direction, "and you mistake yourself Watson," he added. "It was all about the fingernails. The hands, remember? That was the clue to all our riddles, and it is now as plain as daylight. Here! Stop!" he cried to the driver before he could continue.

Holmes opened the cab door, almost jumping out before it came to a complete halt. Handing over a few coins to the driver, he rushed forward and urged me along.

Reluctantly, I emerged back out into the cold, shivering from sudden exposure to the frosty air and hobbled towards my companion who was peering round the corner of the last building in that street, towards our goal.

The Old Brewery was now more visible in the light of day. Amidst the swirling snow and drifting clouds of mist, the chimney rose threateningly over the desolate yard fenced in by a crooked brick wall, encircling the main building that stood looming like a scarlet fortress against the grey sky.

We were retracing our steps from the previous night, walking cautiously into the enclosure through the opening without a gate. The coarse gravel was now covered in snow, and the shallow pits we had discovered in the dark the previous night were now ominously concealed, turning the entire courtyard around the Brewery into a treacherous field.

"Holmes," I said, placing my hand on my companion's shoulder. "Don't you think we should request Inspector Lestrade's assistance in this?" Although I could not help hide the slight quiver which assailed my voice when I spoke those words, it was not out of a sense of utter fear. I felt danger looming around us and my mind and body reacted in the only sensible and natural way possible. Even Sherlock Holmes's footsteps seemed to falter as the desolation around us intensified with every step we took. Our fortunate escape from the hands of those ruffians was only too fresh in our minds. Yet I could not help feel that bringing Augustus and his gang to justice would prove to be something beyond our means, or even the skill of my friend.

"Take heart Watson," he whispered, as we took a few more steps towards the main building. "A client has given us this case and it is our duty to see it through."

Before I could offer any other resistance, we had arrived at the large wooden door that led into the building … it had been left ajar.

I raised my head up towards the high windows which overlooked us, looming like eyes peering from behind a veiled curtain. The structure rose to some five floors and the shape of the brewery made it look like a castle with both sides of the building thrusting out of the main facade where the door stood. On the left, round the corner, lay the ruined shed in which we had hidden.

We were exposed, and the feeling of watchfulness did but deepen. Rising from behind the high roof, the chimney soared high for several more feet. My gaze rose up to its seared and crumbling summit, as flakes of snow drifted into my eyes.

Holmes stood beside me, erect and silent. He looked round with a stern expression on his face, as if gauging the lay of the land in his head and taking into consideration any hidden details that presented themselves to him. Turning back to face the door, he looked at me and gestured towards it.

"Shall we?" he asked.

Suddenly, a loud yell echoed around the Old Brewery. Other shouts joined in, and the rush of footsteps on the thick snow followed soon after.

I was shaken by the sudden appearance of seven or eight men emerging from different points around the brewery, forming a wide circle around us. Holmes and I instinctively moved and stood with our backs against each other, facing the assailants.

They had a rugged appearance and, by the cold, hungry look in their eyes, I did not doubt that we were in the presence of the violent criminals that had pursued us the other night and formed part of Augustus's gang.

Sniggering and harsh coughs came from the men, as they strode towards us bearing bludgeons, pike hooks and knives. We were surrounded by vicious wolves, with no hope of escape.

With all the dangers and suffering we had been through in our attempts to resolve the case, our lives were about to end in a horrible, undignified way. Worst of all, we would fail Miss Harper and these crooks would be allowed to roam free, infesting the streets of London. At that thought my will hardened.

An anger soared within me, a desperate and fierce determination not to die helpless and terrified. I could feel the tense shoulders of Holmes behind me, as he braced himself, ready to fend off the assailants. Suddenly, a door was thrown open and we turned round to face the front of the building, as the men around us paused to look.

A figure in a police uniform stepped forth. I staggered back, seized by renewed fear and consternation, as I recognised the face of the man whom we had pursued all the way there from Warner Street. I had convinced myself that the burly stature of Constable Clarke was the man who had killed Lucy Ward and the gang leader we had identified by the name of Augustus.

Yet, it clearly was not so.

The small frame of the man who had been introduced to me as Constable Shaw, had emerged from the main door. On our first meeting outside Lucy Ward's apartment, I had remarked how young and pale he looked. Yet, the man who stepped silently forward was stalwart, dominating and threatening. Now, the scar across his crooked nose spoke of a life of crime and bloodshed. His clear eyes pierced the very soul with deadly intent. He came out holding a soiled piece of cloth to the side of his bloodied forehead — a wound presumably sustained when he had tripped on the slippery cobblestones.

The nausea I had previously felt suddenly returned and the throbbing pain in my head drummed ceaselessly. The sudden revelation of having been in the presence of the murderer throughout the investigation, made me feel weak and my legs trembled with a mixture of horror and physical strain. Beside me, Holmes had maintained his defiant posture — but I wondered how he had reacted. I recalled he had mentioned nothing of my accusations against Constable Clarke as we chased him out of Warner Street.

"Augustus Shaw," said Sherlock Holmes. "We meet your true self at last."

Shaw winced as he rubbed the cloth against the ugly wound that ran from his left ear up towards his forehead. He grumbled and spat on the ground, throwing away the piece of fabric. He came forward with a smirk — an evil light in his eyes and stopped a few yards before us. Meanwhile, his men drew closer, brandishing their stained weapons fervently in their hands.

The sleeves of his uniform were rolled up and revealed a small tattoo below his right wrist. It was similar in shape and size to the one we had noticed on Phineas Hunter. This one, however, bore a single word:

Deus.

I uttered the word aloud, feeling overwhelmed by the sudden truth.

"I am he, Doctor Watson," he growled. I never recalled having heard that voice come from his mouth, but then again, he had barely spoken those times we met. Although just two days had passed since our first encounter, we were a long way from the caring constable who had reassured his colleague after witnessing the murdered body of Lucy Ward.

"I have taken it upon myself to bring a new order of lawlessness to London," he continued. "These pesky scaremongers and petty thieves that prowl this City are worthless." He looked at his disciples awaiting their master's orders. "These are my subjects, and together we will forge a new future for those who will follow."

"So that justifies the death and persecution of innocents!" proclaimed Holmes.

Shaw smiled.

"I had no enmity towards Lucy Ward. Yet, she became privy to this place and had to be dealt with accordingly," said

Shaw with a sneer. He fingered the knife that was tucked into his belt.

"What of Eleonora Harper? Where is she?" I cried, feeling a hot wrath rising in me. I took a step forward but Holmes stretched out his hand to restrain me.

Shaw looked at us with some surprise.

"Ah yes, the trap you and Mr. Holmes so kindly laid for me at Warner Street. That was very clever indeed." He clapped his hands in mockery.

"You have a very particular way of speaking," said my companion. "For someone so young, living in the criminal squalor of an abandoned brewery, your words are dipped in a sturdy education, which strikes me as highly odd. Unless ..." He faltered, as if some thought or realisation deprived him of words.

"You see, I admire you Mr. Holmes," said Shaw, turning to my friend. "Great man, with a brilliant mind, but too invested in people's emotions."

"I assure you, your assessment on the state of my mind is misplaced," said Holmes, stepping forward in turn. Shaw looked at his men and extracted the sharp knife from his belt.

"After our father died, the inheritance I got was nothing compared to what she had. I pressed her for my share but she refused. The wench!" He gripped the handle of his weapon firmly, as if pained by some past grudge that still held sway on his heart. "So, you see Doctor Watson, as much as I would like to lay my hands on her, I have no idea where my sister is."

"Eleonora is your sister?" I cried in disbelief. My mind went back to the events that had led us to this case, as a helpless woman came to our lodgings in the dead of night — pleading with my friend for assistance to find her missing friend. In her story, she had failed to mention any other siblings, and gave us ample reassurance that she was an only child.

"A truly unfortunate matter," replied Shaw, looking at me with intent.

"Is that why you killed her husband? For your financial gain?" asked Holmes. I looked at my companion, unable to conceal the look of bewilderment on my face at all these revealed secrets. Besides the realisation that Augustus Shaw was Eleonora Harper's brother, I could not fathom how she had been married nor how my friend seemed to know this fact all along.

"The ring, Watson," he said, looking sternly at me. "It was missing from her finger the first time she came to us in that heavy rain. Did you not notice the barest hint of a lighter shade of skin around the fourth finger?"

Holmes turned back to Shaw, relaxing his stiff posture and placing his hands behind his back. The snow, which had momentarily ceased, began falling once more without respite.

"I see your ruse has led you into taking some drastic decisions," he said, gesturing at the uniform.

Shaw made a gurgling sound and spat once more. He tore away the buttoned collar as if the uniform disgusted him.

"The incompetence at Scotland Yard is like a disease. Failure to keep even their own quarters safe is abhorrent. They are a broken structure that is on the verge of collapse. Playing the part of a newly arrived police constable was easy enough to convince even the supposedly astute mind of Inspector Lestrade." He smirked. "I had to keep an eye on the law if I was going to work against it," he winked.

He stepped forward, closer towards us. The knife was held skillfully before him, ready to pierce our flesh. For the first time, I noticed several ragged fingernails on his dirty and mangled hands.

"You escaped from our den once, and yet here you are again. Trapped!" Shaw's wicked laugh filled the air. "Now you know our secret, you cannot leave again." The threatening posture of Augustus Shaw came forward, holding his knife at arm's length. His men too came towards us.

I readied myself as best I could, already locking my gaze upon the first to lay his hands on me.

Holmes took a step back and whistled loudly.

Shouts from further off broke out, accompanied by the baying of dogs and the rushing of footsteps. Whistles rose piercingly above the tumult, as police officers charged into the enclosure, encircling the gang.

Inspector Lestrade marched forth from behind us and ordered his strong force of men forward.

Augustus's men were clearly outnumbered but they were not going to allow themselves to be taken so easily.

Their leader, momentarily distracted by the sudden, unforeseen appearance of the law, paused in his attack. Holmes acted swiftly. He rushed forward, crouching below the short stature of Shaw and pulled at his weapon hand, before swerving round his back and twisting his arm. His opponent was defenceless and he fell to the ground from my companion's solid kick to the back of his knee, throwing him off balance.

The other members were soon apprehended amid much shouting and howling of dogs. Constable Clarke was also present, directing the procedure of the arrests and escorting the men back to the awaiting prison carriages outside the brewery.

"I see Wiggins delivered my message rather successfully," said Holmes heartily, as he handed over his prisoner to two of the officers. He gave me a mischievous grin, as if in recognition of my earlier plea to involve the police.

"As clear as daylight, Mr. Holmes," said Lestrade. "Alright lads, take 'im away," he said, gritting his teeth at Augustus Shaw, "cursed be the day that I ever took you into my ranks. May death find you swiftly before my fury does."

"Come Inspector!" cried Holmes, moving between the two and pulling Lestrade away. "Your anger is understandable and any shortcomings are no fault of yours. I myself was deceived by his ruse. Do not waste yourself with unnecessary bitterness. I would rather you saw to the apprehension of this lot and see that Scotland Yard maintains its high standards."

"Yes of course Holmes," Lestrade nodded curtly. He headed off towards the others — shouting orders as his voice echoed in the emptiness that had settled once more in the brewery yard.

Holmes and I found ourselves in a lumbering cab, as we gradually followed the route back to our lodgings. As I lay back in the seat, watching the grey world outside pass by, he provided some further details to the case upon a few of my pressing queries.

"Remember Miss Harper's burnt letter, Watson? Were not the initials *A.S.* written on that fragment? Who else but *Augustus Shaw*?"

"But the blood on the sofa at 221B," I stammered in disbelief. "Was it not Constable Clarke who had brushed up against it, following Lestrade's wrath?"

"An unfortunate circumstance, I'm afraid. The original smear of blood had come from a stain on Shaw's uniform trousers. Clarke merely smudged his own when he recoiled from the Inspector. I am sure if you were to look at Shaw's uniform you will find a similar smear — probably from having secretly revisited Miss Ward's lodgings in an attempt to hide any telling clues."

The cab rattled on as it made its way back amid the long winding roads towards Baker Street.

"Remember the fingernails?" Holmes continued, "it was a benign enough trait for a constable to keep his hands behind his back at all times. But once my suspicions fell on Clarke and Shaw, upon handing over the uniform I used as a ruse to infiltrate Otto Becker's warehouse, Clarke's hands were impeccable. Meanwhile, Shaw kept his hands concealed during our whole conversation with Lestrade in the sitting-room. Later on we discovered another nail fragment where Shaw had stood the whole time." Holmes paused for a moment before he continued, "the other nail fragments we found were in Miss Ward's apartment, undoubtedly broken off during the murder, and outside Miss Harper's house — when Shaw came to deliver the threatening letter the same day our client came to our lodgings that evening. Really," Holmes sighed, "were it not for the disappearance of Eleonora Harper, this case could have been rather commonplace."

He paused and turned his head round to gaze back through the cab window.

It was indeed a bittersweet conclusion to the whole affair. When death and violence permeate a case like this, I am never too sure whether I should put it in writing or not. However, given the tragic events, I feel I owe it to my readers and the public to present the truth.

At the same time, there was still no indication as to Miss Harper's whereabouts — the only major mystery that still needed to be resolved. Scotland Yard claimed it was still investigating and had as yet no new information.

I was anxious for her welfare and could see that Holmes was too, but it seemed we had arrived at an insurmountable obstacle.

Days passed and Christmas had gone by too. The festivities provided some respite from the dreadful thoughts that constantly passed through my head about the fate of Miss Harper. Holmes was even more reclusive than usual — a feat even I would have considered almost impossible had I not experienced it myself. He took to staring for long hours at the crackling fire under the mantlepiece, or fiddling ceaselessly with the strings of his violin. Conversations ensued when his mind was occupied by some other analysis or experimentation, in which he would explode into a rapturous exclamation of triumph at his success, or a frustrated sigh. On other occasions, he would divulge a long explanation on his processes of arriving at a particular set of results, but of this case he would utter no word.

Chapter 11
The Confession

As I sit down to write the final pages of this most extraordinary case, I am compelled to recall the events which took place some weeks after the brutal murder of Lucy Ward, and the uncovering of Augustus Shaw's barbaric enterprise. Grim as they might be, I feel nonetheless that with the omission of an epilogue of sorts, I would be doing a disservice to my devoted readers.

Inspector Lestrade's reputation within Scotland Yard had seemed dangerously precarious, and on the brink of collapse, following the revelation that one of his recruited constables turned out to be a vicious criminal. Following the successful resolution of the case, news spread like wildfire around London, reaching the ears of some of the highest governmental officials. The authorities were appalled by the infiltration and made a considerable effort to announce to the public that someone would eventually be held responsible for it.

Thankfully, the Scotland Yard inspector was saved from a certain, irrecoverable downfall by my friend's intervention. It soon became known that it was the ever-resourceful and successful Lestrade who had reached a satisfying conclusion to the matter of Miss Ward's murder, and the revelation of the killer's identity. As with numerous other cases, Sherlock Holmes had refused any gratitude or attention for his work, and the Inspector found himself once again in the praise of many of his colleagues and respectable public servants.

Augustus Shaw was duly interrogated, put on trial, found guilty and sentenced to death by hanging on the second day of February, 1896. In addition, the remainder of the then leaderless criminal gang at the Old Brewery was rounded up and brought to justice — the result of a concerted effort by Inspectors Lestrade and Gregson, the latter having temporarily suspended any childish feud between the two, in an attempt to take a share of his colleague's praise.

Despite the gruesome murder and attacks which took place, not least my friend's and my own perilous adventures, it all seemed to end up in the best manner possible. Yet, the biggest mystery of all was the fate of Eleonora Harper. Although her true past had now been revealed, her disappearance during the case was both unexpected and a severe blow to the investigation.

Scotland Yard had come to the conclusion that our client had fled to the safety of another country in the hopes of a better life — away from the persecution of her violent brother.

There seemed to be some truth to this, and yet I could distinctly see that Sherlock Holmes was far from being completely satisfied by this outcome.

As opposed to other cases, there was something in his behaviour which indicated he was vexed by something.

He took to playing the violin almost unceasingly — often finding himself staring out of the window, producing incoherent notes — lost in some deep, dense forest of thoughts only the mind of Sherlock Holmes could conjure.

It was on a fine morning early in January of the new year, that Mrs. Hudson came in carrying breakfast.

Both Holmes and I had been up for a while, idling in the sitting-room, waiting — as if we both instinctively foresaw that some news or other would reach us that day.

As the landlady left the tray on the table, she walked over to my companion, who had just commenced a thorough investigation of several exotic-looking leaves he had extracted from his coat pocket.

"Mr. Holmes, this just came for you and Doctor Watson," she said, placing a small envelope on the desk at which he was sitting.

My companion, consumed by the examinations he was conducting through his magnifying lens, remained silent and made no attempt to offer any remark of gratitude or recognition, leaving an irritated Mrs. Hudson with nothing else to say, except produce an injured groan and a swift departure.

I left the sofa and newspapers I had been going through and went towards the table where the breakfast had been laid.

A few minutes into my second serving of eggs and ham, I looked up at Holmes, still consumed with his analysis of the odd-looking leaves with a variety of green shades.

The envelope remained untouched on the side of the desk. I knew more than to just go ahead and open it. The matter would have to be dealt with delicately.

It was not the first time that Sherlock Holmes impressed upon me the importance of giving him precedence over the opening of such items — even those addressed to both of us.

"Could be important," I said, breaking the heavy silence.

"Or most likely pointless," he replied calmly, keeping his eyes fixed on the specimen before him. "In which case a complete misuse of my time. Time, which at the moment, I most certainly cannot afford to squander away from my current research in favour of some petty thing."

"Its contents could probably be only a short letter or a trivial note," I said, looking at the relative thinness of the envelope. "A few minutes in all," I added.

"In that case Doctor Watson," sighed Holmes, looking up at me, "do take care of the matter yourself if it means sparing me a few more minutes of silence."

He lowered his head again and proceeded in dipping the leafy fragments into a boiling test tube. Meanwhile, I rose from my chair and picked up the envelope. It was made of fine paper, and the hand which wrote the elegant lettering of both our names was certainly accustomed to the refined sophistication of calligraphy.

The writing on the letter inside had the same elegance of a firmly held dip pen, with perfectly composed lines and close attention to each word and punctuation.

Sitting down on the sofa, I read the words aloud:

Greetings Mr. Holmes and Dr. Watson,

It is with a sense of peace and satisfaction that I write out this letter to you. Yet, do not think my gratitude is misplaced. It is partly out of compassion, and regret at my deceitful game, that I send these few words.

I believe I owe you both an apology and an explanation. Let this letter be a testament to the suffering I have endured, the reasons for my actions and the uncompromising truth behind the events you have been drawn into.

With the case now solved, you will have been exposed to the facts that Augustus Shaw is in fact my brother. Following our father's death, we parted ways and he took a deep, dark road into the criminal world. I, on the other hand, found love and respect in Rupert, a man who would become my husband, for a short while.

As our family's coal mining business came to an end, we both inherited our share of my father's fortune, and I looked forward to the prospects of a new life away from our country home. Our mother had died shortly after my betrothal, and it was only through Rupert's caring disposition that I found solace and healing from grief. However, what looked like the beginning of something prosperous, soon turned into a renewed period of anguish.

Not a year had passed since my marriage when Augustus showed up at our house in the country. He looked in a terrible state, smelling of alcohol and tobacco — his mind consumed by anger and violence. He confessed he had used up all his inheritance and demanded some financial aid.

Rupert, a man both proud and not easily daunted by threats, refused him any assistance and sent him away from our house in great wrath. A few weeks later, my husband, who worked in London as a banker, was brutally assaulted and robbed. He was left in a pool of blood upon the street and died shortly after the doctors came to assist.

The news of his death shattered me completely. I was devastated at yet another loss of one so dear. The police came to no conclusion as to the culprit, but I was adamant that my brother was the man behind the heinous attack on my husband.

You see, Mr. Holmes, such suffering changes a person. I had endured pain and grief, and unending trials at barely the age of thirty. I was determined to seek out Augustus and bring him to justice — my own way.

The plan would take time to put into place, but the thought of retribution made me wait until the right opportunity presented itself.

I took up quarters in London on Warner Street, with the pretence of a new life. I watched and waited. I prowled the streets in the guise of an innocent passerby, but my mind *concealed one, unending thought — retaliation. I knew the name of my brother had presented itself on many a quivering tongue in this city's criminal world.*

Within two years, I had established myself comfortably there, and nothing of my past was ever made known to the people around me. But the temporary peace I had gained, was soon disturbed as I crossed paths with Augustus himself. How he sneered and taunted me, knowing that I now lived in London. Old fears and threats came back to haunt me. He made no attempt to deny what he had done to my husband, and still demanded his share of my inheritance, at whatever cost.

That was when I forged a friendship with Lucy Ward.

I was aware from our first meeting that she would be unfairly placed between my brother and myself. She would become the sacrificial lamb for the greater good, which would result in the incarceration of Augustus and the removal of a dangerous criminal from society.

Do not think of me as an insensitive woman. Many a time I found myself not without misgivings about this horrid plan of mine — especially when I got to know Lucy more. Yet, the thought of Rupert unjustly taken away from me overshadowed all else.

I discovered the whereabouts of Augustus's gang by the Old Brewery and asked Lucy to meet me there one evening, when I knew my brother would be present.

The threatening letter I received from my brother that evening was indeed genuine, and yet, when presenting my case to you I could not show you all its contents — given the revelations which lay within and which I wanted to conceal from you. I therefore burnt the first part of the paper, keeping only the last few words and the initials of its author — anticipating that upon its presentation, you would be more willing to pursue the case of a hopeless woman.

I failed to present myself at the meeting with Lucy, hoping she would involuntarily end up being privy to the gang's hiding place, thereby forcing Augustus's hand. After some time, Lucy must have given up waiting for me and a little later I espied her return to her lodgings accompanied by a man, with my brother skulking in the shadows.

Such irony! There I was, on the trail of my brother's murderous path which would surely lead to his own doom. It was on that rainy night that I took the decision to come to Baker Street and seek your assistance. On my way there I realised the bonnet I wore would not aid my illusion of a desperate woman in need of help, which is why I left it upon the pavement before coming up to your lodgings.

What followed in Sekforde Street, I dare not dwell upon. Reading about the savagery with which the murder was committed almost drove me mad with guilt. Yet, the plan was set in motion and I had to see it through.

I knew Augustus would soon seek me out in retribution, which is why I had made plans to leave as soon as the crime had been carried out. From then on, I hoped the case would come to a successful conclusion before Augustus could find out again where I had gone.

Believe me when I say that I never wanted either you or Dr. Watson to be put in harm's way. The acquisition of your services in the investigation of Lucy's death seemed to be a guarantee that Augustus would be caught and duly put on trial. I bear no blame for the terrible events you were to go through and yet, as things turned out, my plan came to successful fruition.

I do hope Celestine has forgiven my sudden absence. She was such a sweet girl and the closest of friends I have had in a long time. Now I must end this letter and leave judgment upon *my behaviour to yourselves. I do hope you look at me in a better light now that you know the truth behind the decisions I took.*

What peace I hoped for in Augustus's death I shall have to discover in some new life I now seek beyond the shores of England. May you both live long enough to put forth your skills and provide comfort to the desperate and hope to those in need.

Sincerely,

Eleonora Harper

"Extraordinary," I said quietly. The shocking revelations which I read out aloud were quite disturbing. Sherlock Holmes, who upon realisation of the letter's author had abandoned his investigation of exotic leaves, stood up and stared silently at the letter I held in my hands.

"So that is why her bonnet was wet that day it was found by the side of the road!" I exclaimed. "Even though there had been no rain since the previous day."

"Correct," said Holmes quietly. "On that night when she came to us in her apparent distress, soaking wet, did you not notice that part of her hair was not as drenched as the rest? Clearly, Miss Harper had left her house wearing that same bonnet on her way to 221B, only to realise that her appearance on our doorstep without the hat would provide for a more convincing story about the disappearance of her friend. Upon arriving here, she abandoned the bonnet by the side of the road to complete her ruse."

Holmes paused, striking a match to light up the contents of the briar pipe he had snatched from the mantlepiece.

"That is the brilliance of the woman, Watson," he said upon a sudden, "and yet, she made one grave mistake." I raised my eyes from the letter in front of me and looked at the stalwart stature of my friend, holding his pipe in hand and staring into the distance towards the window.

"With a sophisticated touch of genius, after you saw her depart that night in a cab from 221B, she returned to retrieve the bonnet. The following day, she left her house and passed by Farringdon Lane, where she dropped the hat and trampled upon it, knowing that its eventual discovery would aid her disappearance, and make it look as if she had been kidnapped."

"Trampled?" I asked, confused by my friend's remark.

"It was transparent. Upon close investigation of the shoe markings, it was evident that someone had purposely stepped on the bonnet — the position of the markings and the clarity of the imprints were unmistakable. It was my first indication that something about Miss Harper's story was amiss."

Sherlock Holmes puffed away at his pipe.

A silence settled in the sitting-room of 221B. I was busy with my own thoughts, pondering the words in the letter and the hurtful deception we had been subjected to by our client — a woman I presumed to be free from all fault in this brutal and unforgiving case.

Yet, at the same time, a sense of fondness and admiration grew in me for Eleanora Harper. Here was a member of the fairer sex who, having sustained her own share of unpleasant experiences in life, managed to outwit a hardened criminal and bring some deserved justice, if at the expense of an innocent individual.

"Well, that's that!" said Holmes suddenly, breaking off my thinking. I looked up at him, standing there gazing at the pipe he was fiddling with. The expression on his implacable face gave way to some sense of misgiving.

The revelations of Miss Harper, though not completely surprising to him, seemed to sow a seed of doubt about his own analytic skills of observation. Whatever he thought of himself, I could not help but realise the humanity which existed in my friend. No matter how uncompromising a character he could be, there lay subtle faults in his otherwise superb intelligence which brought about an earthly quality to his personality and reinforced my idea that beneath that intractable nature of his, there still lay a heart and soul.

"What now then?" I asked, putting aside the letter and sitting up to pour myself another cup of tea.

"The curtain has now fallen on this case," he said quietly. He approached the mantlepiece and placed upon it the briar pipe with its contents still smoking. "If you do intend putting this account into one of your stories Watson, then do so with steadfast clarity. Whatever failings I may have brought to the case, let it be known — so that it shall serve me as a reminder of my own shortcomings."

"I shall endeavour to tell the truth — as clear as it can be," I said, taking a sip of tea, "including the audacious exploits of Sherlock Holmes."

My companion smiled gently but said nothing. He stepped forward and picking up his coat from the armchair, put it on.

"Now you must excuse me Watson," he said, "but I have an appointment with a Mr. Becker at the Shadwell Dock Stairs.

I believe he has a singular blend of tobacco he has promised me a sample of."

He buttoned his coat, nodded curtly, and went downstairs, before disappearing into the exuberant bustle that embellished the interminable character of Baker Street.

Also from James Moffett

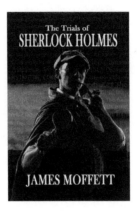

It is a cold London morning in 1887, and the discovery of a dead man in an abandoned house plunges Sherlock Holmes and Dr John Watson into a series of eight trying cases that will test the friendship of the two companions and threaten the safety of the country itself. From a staged murder to an impossible suicide, the theft of a national document to the disappearance of an entire family, London's foremost consulting detective and his faithful companion must seek out the clues and venture into the very heart of each mystery. All the while a sinister force, lurking amid the busy streets of London, stalks their every case, testing their own mental and physical prowess; ultimately they require the assistance of their closest allies, including Mycroft Holmes and the unsophisticated Inspectors Gregson and Lestrade. Will Holmes and Watson be able to avert the approaching threat that appears to be vengefully heading straight for them?

Also from MX Publishing

MX Publishing is the world's largest specialist Sherlock Holmes publisher, with over a hundred titles and fifty authors creating the latest in Sherlock Holmes fiction and non-fiction.

From traditional short stories and novels to travel guides and quiz books, MX Publishing cater for all Holmes fans.

The collection includes leading titles such as _Benedict Cumberbatch In Transition_ and _The Norwood Author_ which won the 2011 Howlett Award (Sherlock Holmes Book of the Year).

MX Publishing also has one of the largest communities of Holmes fans on Facebook with regular contributions from dozens of authors.

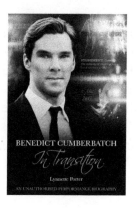

www.sherlockholmesbooks.com

Also from MX Publishing

The Detective and The Woman Series

The Detective and The Woman
The Detective, The Woman and The Winking Tree
The Detective, The Woman and The Silent Hive

"The book is entertaining, puzzling and a lot of fun. I believe the author has hit on the only type of long-term relationship possible for Sherlock Holmes and Irene Adler. The details of the narrative only add force to the romantic defects we expect in both of them and their growth and development are truly marvelous to watch. This is not a love story. Instead, it is a coming-of-age tale starring two of our favorite characters."
Philip K Jones

www.sherlockholmesbooks.com

Also from MX Publishing

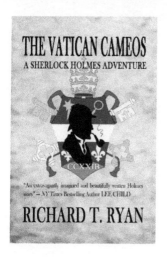

When the papal apartments are burgled in 1901, Sherlock Holmes is summoned to Rome by Pope Leo XII. After learning from the pontiff that several priceless cameos that could prove compromising to the church, and perhaps determine the future of the newly unified Italy, have been stolen, Holmes is asked to recover them. In a parallel story, Michelangelo, the toast of Rome in 1501 after the unveiling of his Pieta, is commissioned by Pope Alexander VI, the last of the Borgia pontiffs, with creating the cameos that will bedevil Holmes and the papacy four centuries later. For fans of Conan Doyle's immortal detective, the game is always afoot. However, the great detective has never encountered an adversary quite like the one with whom he crosses swords in "The Vatican Cameos.."

"An extravagantly imagined and beautifully written Holmes story"
(**Lee Child**, NY Times Bestselling author, Jack Reacher series)

9 781787 053700